FLESHMARKET

Also by Nicola Morgan

Mondays Are Red

FLESHMARKET

NICOLA MORGAN

Delacorte Press

Published by
Delacorte Press
an imprint of
Random House Children's Books
a division of Random House, Inc.
New York

Copyright © 2003 by Nicola Morgan

Originally published in Great Britain in 2003 by Hodder Children's Books

Visit us on the Web! www.randomhouse.com/teens
Educators and librarians, for a variety of teaching tools,
visit us at www.randomhouse.com/teachers

Library of Congress Cataloging-in-Publication Data
Morgan, Nicola.
Fleshmarket / Nicola Morgan.
p. cm.
Summary: In nineteenth-century Scotland, following the death of his mother during surgery, Robbie decides to take revenge on the surgeon who performed the operation, Dr. Robert Knox, and in the process, makes a gruesome discovery about the lengths the medical profession will go to advance its knowledge of anatomy.
ISBN 0-385-73154-X (trade)—ISBN 0-385-90192-5 (GLB)
[1. Medicine—Fiction. 2. Knox, Robert, 1791–1862—Fiction. 3. Physicians—Fiction. 4. Poverty—Fiction. 5. Scotland—History—19th century—Fiction.] I. Title.
PZ7.M82615Fl 2004
[Fic]—dc21
2003011441

The text of this book is set in 11-point Galliard Roman.

Printed in the United States of America

August 2004

10 9 8 7 6 5 4 3 2 1

BVG

With huge thanks to my two experts: Richard Rodger, professor of urban history at the University of Leicester, and the Reverend John Weir Cook, Church of Scotland minister. Their expertise and support were invaluable and any mistakes that remain are my fault. Special thanks to Chris Kloet, my editor, for her enormous influence on the shape of this story, for telling me what I often did not want to hear, and for the inspirational book of old Scots songs. And finally, thanks to my daughters and especially to Harry, my husband, for putting up with it all.

The Doctor

O dinna fear the doctor,
He comes to mak' ye weel,
To nurse ye like a tender flower,
And your wee head to heal;
He brings the bloom back to your cheek,
The blithe blink to your e'e—
An't werena for the doctor,
My bonnie bairn might dee.

O wha would fear the doctor!
His pouthers, pills an' a';
Ye just a wee bit swither gi'e,
An' then the taste's awa'!
He'll mak' ye sleep as sound's a tap,
And rise as light's a flee—
An't werena for the doctor,
My bonnie bairn might dee.

A kind man is the doctor,
As mony poor folk ken;
He spares nae toil by day or night
To ease them o' their pain;
And O he lo'es the bairnies weel,
An' tak's them on his knee—
An't werena for the doctor,
My bonnie bairn might dee.

Alexander Smart

FLESHMARKET

Prologue

Edinburgh, the Infirmary, 1822

The woman walked slowly into the room, her stiff skirts rustling in the sudden silence. A man, in long black coat and firmly pointed collar, came toward her and led her across squeaky floorboards toward the table. He did not look at her face. She did not look at the table.

She kept her eyes down so that she need not study the crowds ranged around the walls of the vast, cold room. More than three hundred people, her husband told her proudly later. All come to watch her operation. All hoping to learn something that would help others.

Her left breast, where the tumor was, swelled against her arm. If she did not have this operation, the tumor would grow and spread and eventually she would die, her lungs rattling with fluid and her bones brittle with pain. She had seen it happen to her mother.

What the surgeon had not told her, in his need to persuade another patient to endure his knife, was that the chances were high that she would die anyway.

Another man came toward her, again not meeting her eyes, his collar squashed into his thick neck and a jewel of moisture on his wispy mustache. He led her to the table.

Behind, her husband carried the baby, two years old, too young to understand. She could hear a dog's scratchy claws tap-tapping on the floorboards, rising above the curious murmurs of the crowd.

"Lie down here. Please," said the man, pointing to the large oak table in the middle of the room. Under the table sat a bucket, half full of pinkish water, with two worn scrubbing brushes nearby. The table was not completely dry.

The woman placed her back to the edge of the table and with her hands tried to lift herself onto it. She had to jump two or three times before she could reach high enough but after some awkward wriggling, in front of all these watchers, she was sitting on the edge of the table. She hoisted her legs up onto it, trying to keep her dignity, smoothing her skirts down and holding her feet tightly together. She shivered and cold sweat chilled her armpits. She lay down on the damp wood, arms rigidly beside her.

She looked at the ceiling and grew colder. A large spider hung briefly on its thread above her face. Watched her watching it. It scuttled back toward the safety of its web. The sunlight threw flickering shadows, which danced drowsily across the dull ivory plaster. The loud murmuring of the spectators lulled her and she could almost believe that this was not going to happen.

No one had spoken her name since she entered the room. Maybe she was not really there? Where was her husband standing? Where was her baby, her curly-haired, diamond-eyed daughter? She was glad her older child, Robbie, had not been allowed into the room. But she must not scream, or he would hear from outside and not understand that this was something that must be done, this cutting into his mother while she lay awake on the table. In front of all these peering bushy-faced men.

Suddenly she heard the sound of the door opening, the hushing, and slow footsteps tapping a smooth semibreve beat across the floor. The dog barked.

"Make that dog be quiet!" came a voice of strange musical richness. It was a young voice, liquid, honey-smooth.

Through glazed eyes, a distant part of the woman's brain took in the man's pockmarked ugliness, his gummed unseeing eye. Yet there was something comforting in this ugliness, something unthreatening. He had been ill treated by life and yet he chose to be here with her, to help her.

The voice continued, from close by her, softly, "You will need to undress yourself. Otherwise, how can I perform my task?" His perfume washed over her. Floral. Roses, sweet, heady.

Obediently, but blushing hot red, she sat up awkwardly. Her breast hurt as her arm brushed against it and she felt again the angry mass of the tumor. She fumbled with the buttons and struggled to free her arms. No one helped. It would not have been proper.

The young surgeon carefully tucked his lacy cuffs out of sight, under his soft mulberry coat, its buttons glinting. He checked that the chain of his timepiece hung in a perfect arc across his front. The other man held an apron for him. The surgeon bent his head and the apron was slipped over his neck and tied behind him.

Unseen eyes wandered over her nakedness. A breath of chill air brushed her exposed chest. She shivered. The room waited.

"Just one side. One side is sufficient," said the surgeon.

She mumbled her apology, as though she should have known. As she lay down once more, half covered now, aware of her own acrid sweat, she saw him take from a deep place within his apron some metal instruments. Three sharp knives and some things like scissors, amongst a fistful of metal objects with unknown purposes.

The woman found herself breathing faster. She did not know anyone who had had surgery before, but she knew that it must hurt. She had tried to imagine how much, had reassured herself by saying, "If someone else can bear it, I can bear it too. It is only pain. We are made to bear pain. Men bear worse than this on the battlefield." Her knees were locked, her lower back arched off the table, her fingers clenched tight as walnuts.

Someone put a thin white cloth, a handkerchief, over her face. She did not know why. She could still see through it. It smelt of moths and tobacco, clinging to her skin like a cobweb. Now several men came closer, two on each side of her. The ghost of a face loomed over hers. She smelt their pipe breath, the dark sweat of their bodies, heard the rustling of their stiff clothes. Strong male hands grasped her wrists and ankles. Fingers held her head. She started to struggle, her breathing fast, her chest bursting.

"Be calm. I have not started yet. Stay very still and very calm. It will soon be over. My usual time is one and three quarter minutes. You can bear it for so short a time. Childbirth takes longer than that. Be very calm and breathe slowly and deeply."

His voice barely reached her terror. She wished someone would hit her on the head, knock her out. Her body was not hers. It pounded with fear. Blood spat through her heart. Air

4

trapped itself in her chest. Her teeth hurt. Tears squeezed between clenched eyelids.

Then, through all this fear came the voice of her baby. "Mammy, Mammy, not cry, Mammy," and tears were in the words. Her mother's love drowned everything else and she turned toward where her baby's voice came from. She spoke from under the cloth.

"Do not fret, little one. Your mammy's well. All is well. I will be with you soon."

Silently she shrank back down into herself and waited for what was to come.

The pain was one shattered scream, shooting into a million splinters in her ears. Something was stuffed between her teeth. Every muscle in her body, every joint, jerked into spasm. Something rasping was inside her, scraping against the bones in her chest, digging into her, tugging, ripping. She felt blood flow around her back and blackness flooded over her, suffocating.

As if in a dream she flew toward a white light, stretched from head to toe on a silver arrow, twisting, unbreathing, spiraling, silent screaming. Somewhere else, down there, behind, was the pain, but she was outside it, watching it and hearing it. As long as she could hold her breath, she would not be down there. She could hold her breath forever, forever and ever and ever. She could stay out here, up here, and never go back. Stay in the knife-sharp angel whiteness, never breathing again. How easy it would be, how dizzyingly easy just to float away. She watched with detached pity the dwarfed figure of herself pinned on the table in the room below, like a beautiful but damaged butterfly specimen not quite dead.

Outside the room, her son, only eight years old, clenched his ears between his hands. He crouched in a ball and rocked and rocked and rocked, to lull the sound of his mother's scream. She saw him from above and reached out for him, held him in her heart, flew with him, floating free together, and then, suddenly, simply, she let him fall. She dropped him. Something closed inside her and she let him go. As he fell alone, a part of her cried for him but did not properly feel the crying. She knew there was a reason for crying but she could not grasp what it was before it had gone. Now she was in a place where nothing seemed as strange as it should.

The arrow reached the top of its path, slowed, hovered, turned and began to arc back down to earth, away from the light and silence. Back to the pain. Dragged into reality, she felt once more the cold hardness of the table. She was burning, ice hot.

Some more tugging at flesh that did not feel part of her, some more clenching of her jaw so tightly that a tooth cracked down the middle, and then the voice said, "Finished. A good job, I believe you will all agree. This woman came to us today with a large tumor of the breast and she will leave us cured of her cancer."

The men around the room clapped and the noise of their admiration rose like wind in a graveyard. The woman was helped to a sitting position by someone. Steadying her dizziness, biting back the sick faintness that threatened to disgrace her, she lifted her legs off the table and stood up. Someone behind her wrapped bandages around the heavy pad that was pressed to the place where her breast had been. She gasped.

Composing herself, the woman stood, curtseyed to the surgeon, curtseyed to the rows of faceless watchers, and followed her husband and baby out of the room. She held her head high but looked at no one.

The dog followed behind, scratch-scratching on the wooden floor.

The surgeon dropped the instruments into the bucket of cold pink water and strolled over to speak to a friend in the audience, wiping his hands on a large handkerchief. A young man picked up the instruments and shook them in the water. He lifted them out again and carried them dripping to the surgeon. Using his handkerchief, the surgeon dried them. He held one knife up to the light for those close to him to see the brilliant sharpness of its blade. He spat on it and polished it on his sleeve. It sent a diamond of light dancing onto the ceiling and everyone laughed when the light landed like an angel on the door as it closed behind the grateful woman.

Footsteps echoed through the towering corridors, as the woman walked, smooth as marble, unbreathing, followed by her silent family. No one could touch her. She touched none of them. She was different. Robbie, young as he was, felt it. He had felt her pain as though it was his. It had burnt him and left its mark. The mark was the empty space where his real mother had been. The place where she had left him.

The first day after surgery, the woman felt weak. An apothecary instructed that she should be kept quiet. The authorities gave special permission for straw to be spread outside the house to deaden the clattering and clashing of hooves and carriages.

On the second day, she felt stronger. She asked for

chicken broth and her husband brought it to her himself, glad to see that she was on the mend. He handed the baby back into her care with relief and went to his work. Important work, which Robbie did not understand but which gave them increasing prosperity and comfort. Robbie, watching his mother constantly, fearfully, was pleased she was getting better too. When his mother was better, everything would be all right again. They could carry on as they had been before. Looking forward.

On the third day, she felt merely tired and somewhat absent. Her breast—or the place where her breast used to be—was painful and red. Hot to touch. Two pink spots flushed her cheeks. The apothecary told her that this was her body healing itself. Her husband was pleased again—her pink cheeks made her look pretty—young and fresh. As a rose.

On the fourth day, she did not know his name. Did not recognize her trembling son with his eyes so wide and wet. Could not care about her baby's hungry cries. Threw her sweat-soaked blankets off, rattled with bone-deep cold, screamed at the snakes writhing before her eyes, vomited, clawed moaning at the blackening rash that crept over her body.

On the fifth day, she died.

1

Six Years Later—February 1828

Robbie lingered. Daylight was disappearing and the February wind needled through the open-weave cloth of his jacket. But he did not want to go home yet. Here, near the Royal Park, the air was fresher, the wind wafting the scent of the sea instead of the pig-swill reek of the Old Town. He stopped to watch the workmen on the new railway, in noisy humor as they finished work for the day. He could just see through the trees the cavernous hole in the hillside, where each day more rock, blasted by gunpowder, was carried away by horse-drawn rail wagons.

He turned his collar up and hunched his shoulders, thrusting his fists into sagged pockets. He wondered if his father would be home. No point in wondering if he would bring any food, or money. There had been a time—and it seemed a long time ago—when Robbie had relied on his father, when it seemed as though the three of them could manage together. The fire had destroyed more than buildings. It had changed everything. Again.

If it had not been for the fire, Robbie would have had better work than ferrying deliveries for a baker. And a better life to go with it.

He shivered. His sleeves were too short and the material thinned by use. He was hungry. He had bread in his pockets, of course—a whole fresh bannock, still warm. Mr. Brown had given it to him. But Robbie would not eat it until he came home and could share it with Essie and their father.

Robbie's work was done for the day, his last delivery—to the Sheep Heid tavern in Duddingston—safely unloaded and the barrow returned to the bakery near the palace. The looming peak of Arthur's Seat towered behind him and he remembered, as he could not avoid doing each time he passed this spot, the bonfire that had enflamed the sky for King George's visit. But he pushed it from his mind. It was a time better forgotten completely.

He should go home.

He made his way quickly toward the Old Town, leaving Holyrood Palace behind him, its windows yellow and warm, music faint within its walls. Darkness fell more heavily and dank perpetual smoke clogged the air. Shadowed people scurried through the unlit streets. Tall black buildings swooned over him and the stench increased. The cobbled pavements were slippery with filth and rotten food. Doorways and corners seethed with bundles—humans lying wrapped and waiting to sleep. Or drunk. Something fell from a window high above, landing with a splash a few feet in front of him. He hurried on through the thickening darkness.

Voices. Laughter from behind him. He turned. Two figures were rounding a corner and were approaching through the gloom, their way lit by a boy carrying a swinging lamp. Gentlemen, Robbie could see that straightaway. Tall hats, elegant canes waving, dark coats falling almost to their knees, stiff upright collars, their necks warmed by thick cravats. One slapped the other on the back with another roar of laughter. Robbie stood aside to let them pass, pressing himself into an empty doorway. The boy ran along in front, the lamp in one hand and a stick in the other, checking for sudden dips or loose cobbles that might catch the gentlemen's elegant feet.

The taller one, Robbie could see now as they passed, wore a plum-colored coat, lace cuffs flopping from the sleeves, every button gleaming. A jeweled brooch at the throat.

Suddenly, one voice, harsh as cymbals, rang out above the other city noises. A sentence, a name, that made Robbie's blood freeze.

"Gad's sake, Dr. Knox! Keep your flesh-cutting knife away from me! I could not bear such pain!"

Robbie shrank back into his doorway. His breath stuck in his throat. He felt himself spinning backward into a dizzy past that he preferred to forget. No longer fourteen, he was eight years old again, bewildered. He was standing outside a room, a huge black studded door blocking his way. He was alone. Everyone else, his whole world, was on the other side of the door and no one had explained why. He heard footsteps along the chilled marble corridor and saw two men striding toward him, until they were towering over him. One of the men had a monstrous face, gouged and pitted by smallpox. Robbie turned away.

"What is this?" asked the pitted man.

"The woman's child, Dr. Knox," replied the other.

The pitted man bent down, till his face was close to Robbie's and Robbie could smell his perfume. Flowery. "Well, well, young man. Look at me. Come on, look at me. You do not mind my face, do you? What does it matter about my face when I intend to save your mother? Eh? Besides, just look at this coat. Quality. Sheer quality. Took delivery of it only yesterday. Wearing it especially for your mother's operation." He made a tiny adjustment to the way his coat sat, flicked an invisible something from its breast, breathed in more deeply, pumped out his chest.

Robbie found himself oddly drawn to the man's voice, with its warm musical quality. He looked at the face again. It was stiff, like a mask. Then Robbie noticed something else. One eye was white and blank, dead, unmoving. It was frightening because it could be thinking anything. It looked like veined pig fat. He looked away again.

Dr. Knox stood up. "Well, well. Must not keep the patient waiting. How do I look, Hamilton?"

"Superlative, Dr. Knox. As always. No one would guess you had come straight from a cadaver."

Dr. Knox smiled and looked at his fingers for a moment, holding them away from him to focus better. "Onward, Hamilton. Goodbye, laddie."

The door opened, an orchestra of voices rose and hushed as it closed, and Robbie waited. He did not know what for. He strained to hear through the shut door. Nothing. Then perhaps a murmuring rustling, a dog barking, a voice, possibly Dr. Knox's voice, silence.

Then Robbie's world was shattered.

The scream was a blade that sliced through him and he joined it, screaming himself as he rocked and rocked and rocked the scream away. Yet he would never rock that scream away. As he floated tumbling in his mother's arms through the lightest whitest void, holding her tightly, never wanting to let her go, she dropped him, without warning, pushed him away, and when he finished spinning he found himself alone. Alone in front of the closed door, with his hands over his ears. His mother had left him.

Now, just as suddenly, he was back in the present again, back on an Edinburgh street, six years later, seeing two gentlemen walk past laughing. One of them was Dr. Knox. The surgeon. Six years older too, more bushy-faced, grown more into his skin. The lyrical laughing voice echoed in Robbie's head. The memory of that awful moment had been buried deep in the silt of his mind until now. Occasionally over the years he had heard the man's name but seeing him in the flesh, hearing that voice again, made everything different, and real. He followed them, drawn by an inexplicable fascination. He could hear snatches of words, their voices swelling, ripe with claret.

Dr. Knox was speaking now. "A shocking idea, my dear fellow, shocking. To eliminate pain in surgery? Pain is God's will, God's gift. How could we mere mortals be so bold, so dreadfully audacious, as to consider trying to go against God's will? Pain? We must welcome it, as God's gift to us." Knox was flinging his lacy arm in the air as he spoke.

Robbie's thoughts spun like oatmeal in the wind. This was something he had tried not to consider. It was too enormous, too confusing for his mind. God was good and yet God had made his mother suffer and had killed her. God had chosen to take his mother from him. And that was God's gift to him. He had heard this message many times before. In the kirk each Sunday, until they stopped going four years ago, and now in the streets sometimes, listening to the preacher in his wooden tent, ranting to a rowdy crowd about God's will and punishment and salvation. And damnation.

Robbie could not think of blaming God. Could not hold such a terrible thought in his head for fear that lightning would strike him dead, or typhus, or the plague sent as a punishment. Was his poverty not already a sign of God's anger with him and his family? That was what the clever preachers said. That poverty was a fair punishment. Somewhere in Robbie's mind a tiny doubt occasionally fluttered, but every time he squashed it dead. Doubt was a sin.

So, he dare not blame God. But what about this man, this Dr. Knox? Surely he was to blame? This was the evil man who had killed his mother. And from his mother's death had come the destruction of her family's dreams. It had been the beginning of the end. Of course, there had been the fire, but first there had been his mother's death. It had changed his world. Yet this man, the cause of it all, this doctor, neither knew nor cared. Here he was, now, six years later, still caring nothing of what he did to people. How could he swagger around in his expensive clothes, while others lived like pigs in filth and stench, their lives hopeless?

The other man was speaking now.

"They will not mind so much, Knox, your patients. Most of your patients are dead before they reach you. One could even say that they have the patience of the dead."

Dr. Knox roared with laughter and stumbled against his companion as he slipped in the slime. "How very true, sir. But I treat them all with equal respect. Dead or alive, they all receive my utmost care and attention. However, it is worth noting that it is the living ones who make the most noise. By

Gad! All that screaming—it is surely enough to turn me deaf as well as half blind. Now, if some of these doctors with their fairy-tale ideas of killing pain could stop a patient's noise, there would be something worth paying for."

Robbie's heart pounded. He had to follow them. He could not have said why, only that it was impossible not to. If Robbie's life was a prison, Dr. Robert Knox was the man who had hurled him into it and thrown away the key with a careless pockmarked sneer. Robbie was drawn to him like any enemy to another.

Following a man in the shadowed streets was not difficult. Tiny alleys, unexpected corners and deep doorways made easy hiding places if necessary. There were other people on the street too, some hurrying home before the darkness fell completely, others lingering for their own reasons. Even if Dr. Knox and his companion had looked round, they would not have seen him. He kept his eyes fixed on the two hats a few steps ahead.

He thought of nothing other than following this man and then . . . Nothing else. No clear thoughts, just an instinct, a feeling of being pulled. He did not notice the chill darkening wind, the cold smurring rain across his face. He forgot that his young sister would be waiting for him, on her own if his father was not there.

The two men turned left. Robbie followed them up a short steep street. He knew where he was. There was Infirmary Street in front of him. And there the hospital where . . . He put the thought from him quickly. They turned left, through some gates. Past the hospital, between the shoulders of buildings, they passed into a tree-frothed square. Surgeons' Square. Calm, peaceful, enclosed. Detached from the rotting streets. Secret. The windows like eyes looking down. The carvings above the doors like noses.

Robbie stayed in the shadows of the buildings at the entrance to the square. He watched the men and their boy cross the square and go toward a building in the left-hand corner. They gave something to the boy and he ran off, past where Robbie hid, and out of the square. In front of the men, the door opened, spilling its orange light onto the steps. They went in and the door closed behind them. Now the square was empty.

As wind rustled the trees that grew in the square, whispering, the glow from the gaslights danced lazily across the cobbles. The pavements were swept clean. No bundles in doorways here.

Robbie looked at the building. Was it where Knox lived? It did not look like a square where people lived. The buildings seemed too severe for homes. On this one, the shutters were closed, as if it had folded its arms against him. As he walked carefully toward it, keeping to the shadows at the edge of the square, he saw that light was coming from a gap in the shutters of a basement window. Glancing in all directions to make sure he was not watched, he ran over and looked down through the railings. As he squinted between the gap, it was hard at first to make out what he was seeing. But when his vision adjusted, he gasped.

He could hardly believe what he saw. He moved his head to the side to see more of the scene through the crack. On a table, spread, pinned, exposed, lay, flat on its back, the body of a man. He could not see the legs, but it was clear that it was human. Now, its waxen yellow flesh hardly resembled any man Robbie had seen.

One hand was fixed to the table, palm upward, crucified by tall pins. Flaps of its flesh were peeled away, to show purpled lines and a maze of tiny tubes. One eye was missing. But, no! Not missing, just lying on the table beside the body, sliced open to reveal the jelly inside. Most horrible of all— Robbie held his arm over his mouth and breathed through his sleeve—a huge rectangular hole had been cut in the man's belly. From inside it spilled . . . Robbie could not look anymore.

He turned and ran, his lips clamped together to keep the scream inside. Out of Surgeons' Square, past the hospital without looking or breathing, or thinking, back down the steeply sloped street, across the Cowgate again and into a narrow alley. He felt safer in the familiar darkness of the side roads, away from carriages and people.

As he ran up the filthy narrow street, the same thoughts spattered his brain: What sort of evil was this? What sort of man could cut up a human body in this grotesque ungodly way? What would the pain feel like, when living flesh was sliced and pinned like an insect? And how could his mother not have died of such pain?

Only when he reached the low entrance to his own close off the High Street did Robbie stop running. With his hands on his knees, he bent over, gasping, saliva pooling in his mouth. He spat. He turned into the tiny passageway between the buildings. Hearing a noise, he looked down. A rat stared up at him, its thin lips snarled back, its two top needle-sharp teeth crossed over each other like swords. He kicked it away from the pig carcass that it had been eating. That was probably one of the pigs that lived on the ground floor of Robbie's building. Two adults, nine children and four pigs.

Or three pigs now. One room. The sewage sludging past their doorstep. And swirling around their tiny smoke-grimed window hummed the smell of it, mixed with the rotten meat stench from the entrails and carcasses of the flesh market that by day filled the bottom of the close and gave it its name. Fleshmarket Close. Often a dog or scrawny cat would drag a stolen pig's ear or the hairy meatless end of a cow's tail to the relative quiet of their staircase and chew it before leaving the remains to the rats and flies.

Knox would not be living somewhere like this. Nor would Robbie if his mother had not died.

At the shared stairs to the upper floors, Robbie scraped his boots against the bottom step. Exhaustion hit him then and his thigh muscles were shaking as he climbed to the top floor. There was no light but he knew the way by heart, though he still walked carefully, in case something lay on the stairs. He paused and took deep breaths before opening the door, aware that he did not have much food in his pocket.

" 'S Robbie," he called. Footsteps and scuffling inside as the door opened. Essie's birdlike eyes were diamond-bright, in an eight-year-old's face polished acorn-brown with dirt. Her wiry arms were never still and her grubby dress hung off her scrawny body. Essie had the energy of a sparrow. She survived on sparkle. And she could steal like a magpie. Robbie smiled as he moved his hand to touch her wild dark tangle of hair. She wriggled away and screwed up her face.

"Pleased to see me, Essie? Or pleased to see supper?"

"Supper!" Robbie gripped his sister's hair and playfully tightened his fist. "Supper, supper, supper!" shrieked Essie. "What's for supper?"

"A feast fit for a king," proclaimed Robbie, letting her go. "Guinea fowl, freshly caught from His Lordship's estate, jugged hare in a rich plum sauce with brandy and capers, flavored with herbs from distant parts of the Orient, delicious strawberries . . ."

"You mean bread? An' tatties?" asked Essie.

"Yes, all right, I mean bread. But not potatoes. Sorry. Is he back?"

Essie knew who Robbie meant. She did not answer. "I got milk. It's warming by the fire." She went to fetch what they needed for their meal. Bread and milk. And, as always, oatmeal. Not much. February was the worst time to be poor. Food was scarce and expensive.

Their father often did not come back. Sometimes he disappeared for a week at a time. More than once, he disappeared for a month. There was usually a reason. Twice he had been taken by the army press-gang and had been lucky to escape. Once, Robbie wondered if he had been in prison. Sometimes, his story was that he was trying to find work, but Robbie had stopped believing that anyone would give him any work worth having. Not with the smell of whisky on his breath and the empty wild tired look in his eyes.

Years ago, before . . . when their mother was alive, Robbie's father had been respected. And, for a time, almost wealthy. He had made sufficient money through brains, hard work and a good education. He had gone into business with some friends and been lucky, though lucky was not how it seemed looking back. Insurance, that was the new craze. People were getting rich in insurance and the opportunities seemed endless. A new world, people called it, and Edinburgh at the forefront. Edinburgh still was, and many of those people still were rich. But for every one who had moved into grand spacious squares in the New Town, there were others who had lost everything. Robbie's father was one of those. Without rich friends in powerful places, lawyers or professors, when his business failed he had no one to help him.

Robbie and his family should be in the New Town now, not in this stinking midden. That had been the plan. And how near they had come to it. Before . . .

Now, as they dunked their bread in warm, slightly tangy milk, hunched near a smoking fire in one drafty room at the top of a five-story building, Robbie could not help noticing the plaster crumbling with dampness, the sticky black soot that coated every surface in the room, the crazy muddled shelves of half-broken objects and the endless sickening smell of dead rats under the floorboards and their own waste in a bucket. One bed between three of them, two stools, a table with a broken leg leaning against the wall, water to be queued for and carried up the slippery stone stairs. In February at least there was clean water to be had but in the summer the public well often ran dry and they eked out a jug of stagnant liquid that grew black with flies. They were always hungry, always exhausted, always weak. In winter their eyes were hollow and their skin flaky under their hair. And itchy. Their spit was black with the smoke that hung over the town. This was not a life. An animal could make a better life for itself than this, thought Robbie.

Essie could smile through it. But Essie knew nothing different. Essie had not had time to dream before their mother died.

That night, as the city slumped into silence in the streets far below, and as the two of them lay head to toe in the bed

20

they shared, and as Essie slept, Robbie found his mind wandering to a time that usually he preferred to forget. Now, with his resentment stirred by the unexpected encounter with Dr. Knox, he let himself remember the life that had been taken from him. The life he should still have.

2

A Dream Fit for a King

August 1822. He would never forget it. The city swarming with excitement at King George's visit. Color and heat and noise.

Everything, every detail, was organized by the famous writer Walter Scott. Robbie remembered his father explaining that the visit had been Mr. Scott's idea in the first place. "It is the first time for two hundred years that a British king has come to Edinburgh," said his father proudly as they watched the preparations. "Mr. Scott says it is a way of bringing the Highlanders and Lowlanders together. We live in a new Scotland, Robbie, and Edinburgh is at the forefront."

The streets, scabbed dry by weeks without rain, were now swept clean by gangs of sweating men. Dozens of carts dragged sand from Portobello beach and spread it on the cobbles. Mr. Scott's orders, said Robbie's father, to muffle the sounds of horses and allow the bands to be heard. Each day the town criers announced new orders from the great man. Residents to empty their chamber pots and buckets every morning into the public drain, not the cobbles below. Privies, where they existed, to be emptied too, not left until they overflowed. Every window facing a street to have a light shining in it after dark. No jostling during the King's presence. Each bystander to choose a place and stay in it—no pushing.

Mothers rushed to make new dresses for themselves and their daughters. Men who might find themselves in the presence of the King assembled their uniforms—all to a new design, ordered by Mr. Scott, of course. Tight white breeches, white waistcoat and blue coat, with a blue-and-white cockade on a low-crowned hat, to be decorated with heather.

Strange wild-looking men with enormous manes of shaggy red hair swaggered about, swirling in kilts. At first Robbie was frightened by these creatures—everyone had heard about the terrible behavior of Highlanders. But Mr. Scott had invited them, said his father. "Why do they wear skirts?" asked Robbie. "I am not sure that I know," said his mother. "People are saying that it is all Mr. Scott's idea." Essie hid in her mother's proper skirts as these creatures rolled roaring past, speaking a foreign language of frightening coarseness.

A new wonder—gas lighting. Robbie's father had taken him to watch one day as work began on installing three hundred lights from Holyrood Palace to Dalkeith, the route the King would take each day of his visit. For not a moment of the King's stay must he be in darkness.

A woman who lived near Robbie had been given a special ticket by the provost. She had been chosen to parade on a balcony reserved for the most beautiful ladies. They were to stand and smile and be smiled at by the King. There was excitement, mixed in no small part with jealousy. Was her nose not slightly too thin? Were her shoulders not somewhat rounded? And everyone knew that the roses in her cheeks were not from God but came from her pinching her face whenever she thought no one was looking.

Scaffolding sprouted up the sides of every building. People who lived on top floors sold tickets for others to perch on roofs. When a half-finished scaffold collapsed amid mangled bones and broken heads, and left two young men dead, within a few hours the platform was higher than before.

No one knew which day the King would arrive at Leith harbor, and rumors spread like typhus. Every day more people arrived in Edinburgh: Highlanders, Lowlanders, each suspicious of the other. Traders came from London, selling new essentials, their confident manners a marvel to everyone. Strange accents mingled and voices were loud with excitement. The terrible skirl of bagpipes pierced the air and the city heaved with heat and sweat and breath.

Still, the King had not arrived.

There was another rumor. Robbie's mother was worried: she had heard of a highly unpleasant disease, the Itch, which could be caught from close contact with crowds, especially during celebrations. "But we need not worry," she told her husband. "There is a cure." And she showed him what an English trader had sold her that day as she walked along the Grassmarket: Barclay's Original Ointment. "It has come all the way from England, from London no less," and she gazed wonderingly at the shiny white jar with its clean smooth lid and its elegant, confident lettering.

It was a time for excitement, a time to believe things out of the ordinary.

Then one day, as hot and heaving and noisy as the others, Robbie's father announced that they were going on an outing. A surprise. His mother's eyes shone. They had to put on their best clothes. Two-year-old Elizabeth, Essie for short, had her unruly black curls forced inside a cap and her pinafore changed for a clean one. She fidgeted in her clean white stockings and soft child's slippers. Robbie felt tall and proud in his new grown-up clothes: an iron-brown coat above fawn breeches that stopped just below his knees, and silk stockings that wrinkled at the ankles despite being held up with garters. His new shoes were a little too big and the stockings slippery, so that he had to curl his toes and shuffle slightly to stop them sliding.

They set off, through the bustle and noise. And the color! Robbie did not know a word for it. It was more than the colors of the rainbow. Sunlight reflected from the reds, the blues, the whites, of clothes and flags and carriages. Ostrich feathers dyed every shade imaginable danced from vendors' barrows and ladies' heads. As they walked toward Princes Street, over the sweeping arches of North Bridge, and as they gazed across at the pale buildings on the other side, the city looked carved out of sand. Sunlight streamed across the pillars and spires and copper domes as though heaven was smiling on this city. To the west, the soft hills cupped it in the hands of God. In the other direction rose Calton Hill, its sides swarming with tiny people struggling to the top to see the herring-silver strip of sea where the King would land. Tents were pitched on slopes, so that people would not miss the spectacle when the King came. And to each side of Robbie and his family lay the twin protrusions of the castle rock and Arthur's Seat, two sleeping giants guarding them. There could be nowhere like it in the world.

"Hurry, Robbie," said his mother as Robbie lingered to look. "We have a surprise for you." They were heading toward the symmetrical lines of the New Town.

The surprise was a house. A house sitting in the sun, its

black railings shiny, its iron gate open, clean steps going up to the black door, and others going down to a basement. Robbie's mother and father stood together. His hand rested on her back. A tiny sweat shone on her nose. Her cheeks were poppy-bright, her face fragile, as though she might melt away.

"Who lives here?" asked Robbie, not sure why they were there.

"No one lives here," smiled his father, looking proudly at the house. "It is not ready. But when it is finished, we will live here."

Robbie hardly knew what to think. He wanted to see inside. "May we go in?" How could he live in a house like this, with its own door, and big windows gulping in sunlight? And no filth on the street. A wide street with air flowing through it. Saxe-Coburg Place, it was called, which spoke to him of royalty and foreign courts.

"No, Robbie," said his mother. "Not yet. But you can look through the window." Part of him wanted to run up the steps as a small child might, and stare and stare in wonder. But the other part of him, the one stiff and grown-up in a formal collar and breeches, held back. He walked carefully up the steps, his shoes slipping at the heels and slapping on the stonework. Looking through the railings to the side, he could see into the nearest room on the ground floor. Try as he might, he could not stop his eyes opening wide. It was huge! The ceilings high, the plaster flowing in teardrops around the corners. An enormous fireplace, surrounded by a white carved frame, much wider than the fireplace itself, a ledge above it. The clean straight lines perfect.

He could not imagine living in this house. And yet, the more he thought about it, the more he could see them here, breathing in the space in the huge light rooms.

27

Essie was wriggling in her father's arms. She was not interested. They walked back toward the Old Town, toward the cluster of ramshackle buildings clawing their way up toward the castle. Toward the thick yellow pall of smoke that clung like phlegm to the roofs. Robbie was full of questions and he shared his parents' excitement as they answered and added information of their own. They would have water running from a tap in the kitchen, and their own privy outside. Robbie and Essie would no longer share a bed. They would have servants, two, perhaps even three. Gaslights of their own, fixed to the walls in glass globes, his father explained. A garden, with flowers. Roses—his mother wanted roses.

Robbie's mother looked at his father with pride. This was all due to his success in business, his hard work and his education, she told Robbie. Robbie listened with only a part of himself. He was not interested in how. All he felt was the pure excitement of moving to a new life. Not that he had ever particularly disliked the one he had before, but even he could see now that his old street was narrow and smelt of pigs and fish, while this new one flowed with air from the sea and the hills.

That evening, humid and sticky, they dressed in their best clothes again. Not Essie. Essie was too young. A neighbor came to look after her. Robbie's mother looked fragile as eggshell, in her new silk dress with its skirts the lightest blue of a morning sky. His father stood stiff and proud, rich in plum purple, his arms behind him and his shoulders pulled back, his chin pushed upward by his thick cravat. And Robbie itched in his sharp-edged collar, the new shiny-buckled shoes now painful where they had rubbed skin away.

A concert. Robbie had never gone to a concert before

and was not entirely sure that he wanted to. "This is what we will do when we live in the New Town," explained his father. When we live in the New Town. It was a phrase Robbie had heard a dozen times that day. It still sounded far away.

St. Cecilia's Hall. A short squalid walk from their street, along cobbles newly cleaned for the Visit, but with the smell merely disturbed and the gutters still overflowing with waste. Robbie's mother hoisted her skirts high above the filth with both hands. Ladies held bottles of smelling salts to their noses as they passed. Robbie's mother had some too, and she let her skirts fall to wave the bottle hesitantly beneath her nose, wrinkling it in surprise.

They jostled into the hall. Robbie could not see in this crowd of adults. "Follow me," said his father, and with his mother urging him on he pushed blindly through all the people, until they came to the edge of the room. His father helped Robbie climb onto the ledge that formed the base of one of the many half-pillars that were set into the side of the hall, and he leaned into the space between the pillar and the wall. Now he stood taller than his father and could scan the seething sea of people. He could see the orchestra in their places, lights dancing from their instruments. His father stood close so Robbie could not fall. Robbie could smell his hair, with its warm powdered grease. His mother stood beside her husband, her face shining. She looked hot. But she smiled at Robbie through the noise.

A man was walking to the front of the orchestra. "The conductor!" whispered his father. The audience hushed and calmed. An eager breathless silence. The conductor raised his arms. And then began an evening Robbie would never forget. Sometimes he closed his eyes to the music and let it just flow through him. But most of the time he watched. He gazed at each instrument and tried to identify the sound it made, tried to imagine that he was the player.

But he did not really imagine himself as a player, did not properly feel the pull, until the music shrank to a whisper and amidst the waves of applause another man came out and stood in front of the conductor. This other man, with wild stormy hair and a long neck, dressed all in stiff black and white, held a violin, its rich amber warmth glowing in the lamplight. After a pause, the man bent his body toward the instrument and into the silence he began to play.

Robbie sank into the song the violin sang. He could no longer smell his father's hair, feel the stiffness of his own new collar. He flew with the music, the sad-sounding up-and-down swelling of notes whose names Robbie did not know. Sometimes the notes were tiny, fast, the player's fingers flickering over the strings like spiders' legs. Sometimes they were long and sad and lingering, hovering on each note forever. They flowed from him and through the violin and into the air, where they hung like mist. It could not be an instrument of wood and gut, this violin. It had a voice. The voice of a swan, long and white and untouchable.

After the concert, as they pushed their way into the night air, Robbie was dazed.

"Did you enjoy it, Robbie?" asked his father.

"What was his name?" asked Robbie.

Felix Janiewicz. The name was too spiky, too sharp to make such music. But Robbie wanted to play the violin like Janiewicz.

"How I would like to play the violin like him!"

His father laughed as they began to climb the stairs to their home. His mother smiled, a wisp of damp hair dangling from the coils around her head. "Would you like to learn, Robbie?"

He could only nod. She looked at her husband. "He could, could he not? We can afford it now."

"Of course," said his father. "You may have lessons when we live in the New Town." When we live in the New Town.

"Oh, surely we could start a little sooner than that, my dear." She smiled at her husband. Her silk skirts were drooping now, crushed and limp from the hot crowds.

"Anything for you, my dearest," said Robbie's father.

Robbie sang within.

Inside their small dark home, Robbie's mother stroked sleeping Essie's head and thanked the neighbor.

"You look tired," her husband told her.

"I am a little," she agreed. She did. She looked pale, even yellow-tinged. Robbie thought nothing of it at the time.

The next day, King George's ship was sighted from Leith. But the weather was wild—rain and wind after days of heat. The ship could not land.

His mother took Robbie to a shop. A violin maker's shop. John Blair, stated the sign on the window. A balding, worried man with tiny wire spectacles produced instruments of different sizes and fitted them under Robbie's chin. He made Robbie hold his left arm out straight to see if he could cup the end. He told Robbie that this part was called the scroll. A three-quarter-sized violin was what was needed, decided the man, warming to his task, squinting at Robbie's neck, his fingers, his chin. He had long arms, said the violin maker. Then Robbie had to choose which one.

"They all look the same to me," said his mother.

Later, Robbie would learn that this was because Mr. Blair modeled his violins on those of the great maker Stradivarius. But even on that first day, they did not look the same to him. All were a yellow color, but each with its own features, its own shading and swirling. He touched every one, passing his finger over the shininess until his hand settled on a particular instrument. It spoke to him when he touched it.

To choose a bow, he had to hold the violin and sweep a bow across the strings. The noise was terrible, wiry, and his heart sank. "Dinnae worry, lad, ye'll soon learn," smiled the violin maker. "Everyone mak's sic a sound a' first."

Robbie left the shop with his mother, the beautiful violin safely in a box. He could hardly speak.

Before they went home, his mother stopped at another shop. Her eye was caught by something in the window. "A kaleidoscope, Robbie! I have heard of these. It is the new toy. Would Essie not love one? Shall we buy her one?" Robbie looked through it, amazed at the endlessly different patterns of every color in the world. Kaleidoscope—that was the word he had wanted to describe the colorful words yesterday. More than the colors of the rainbow.

They bought one for Essie and returned home clutching their parcels.

Robbie's mother brushed against the doorway as they went into their home. She winced, stopped, breathed hard. "It is nothing, Robbie. Do not fret," she said.

He was not fretting. He was thinking about his first violin lesson.

That night, the long-awaited bonfire lit up the rain-soaked sky over Arthur's Seat. With the peak invisible against the dark, the glow from the bonfire hung suspended as if by

God. They stood outside with everyone else, hours past their bedtime, and watched the firelight in the sky. Finally, a miracle. Even Essie stood still and watched. Above the invisible chimney of the Edinburgh Gas Company, a ring of fire in the shape of a golden crown hung above the city. Was this God's greeting to the King? Everyone agreed that this was the time, this was the place to be alive.

A month later, without Robbie's understanding why, his mother had died. From that day everything had changed. There was the fire as well, of course, and their father's bankruptcy, but they came later. It was his mother's death that had begun their downfall. And it was Dr. Knox who was responsible for it.

Now, lying cold in bed next to Essie, in their one stinking room on a top floor, the fifth, with stench from below and the rain seeping in from above, it was impossible not to blame the man who had caused it all. Gone was the dream of a beautiful house in the New Town, with its airy rooms in summer and views of distant snowcapped hills in winter. Gone was Robbie's schooling, though he had kept his books and still studied them when he could. As for Essie, she never went to school. She could have gone to a kirk school, except that they did not go to the kirk anymore. Their clothes would not have been acceptable. Besides, said their now-dissolute father when furious with whisky, his voice no longer English-sounding but settled in the Scots of his birth, "God has decided who gaes to heaven and who doesnae—wha' difference would it mak'? He mak's it fair plain wha' He thinks o' us."

Robbie was worried by this thought. Frightened of how

it seemed to match the dark fear lurking inside him. Frightened of what it meant for the future. Because God decided everything. Did He not? What would God think about them not going to the kirk anymore? Perhaps He would decide to punish them further?

There was something else that Robbie had lost. He would never forget the day. Maybe a year after the fire, with no money in the house, and more often than not no food on the table, he had come home from his job selling salt around the wealthier houses. He opened the door to their room. He noticed immediately. His eye was drawn straight to the empty place.

"My violin!" he whispered. Essie looked at him and turned away, her lips tight, her eyes slitted with worry. "Where is my violin, Essie?" he shouted now. Footsteps on the stairs. His father, red-faced with exertion, weak from the climb, leaned against the door frame bleary-eyed.

"Where's my violin?" demanded Robbie.

"Food, will ye look?" said their father. "Guid food. Breed, and a whole chicken. Apples. Ale for ye, Rabbie— ye're auld enough now."

"Where is my violin?"

"Would ye no' raither ha'e food?"

Then Robbie knew. His father had sold the violin for food. As he watched Essie hungrily swallowing her supper and his father's eyes gleam as he drank whisky from a cracked glass, the last glass they had, he knew then that this must be the end. The end of any dream.

Three years later, Robbie was usually careful not to dwell on thoughts of what his life might have been like. Tonight, however, as he lay next to curled-up Essie, trying not to think about the emptiness in his stomach, he made no effort to stop himself. Something murky stirred in the silty depths of his mind.

Was it seeing the hospital again? Was it hearing the cello sounds of Dr. Knox's voice? Or was it seeing that dissected body bare and split open?

It was seeing Knox, surely? Seeing the man who was the cause of it all and discovering that this man did not know or care what he had done to Robbie and his family.

He felt tears begin to squeeze between his eyelids. He knew there was only one way to drive away these tears. Anger. He heated up the anger he needed, till it boiled. Soon, he could form the anger into a thought. Somehow, anyhow, Dr. Robert Knox must know and pay. Know just what he had done, and be sorry for it.

Robbie slept. Tomorrow he would act.

3

Caught

Their father had still not come back by morning. Robbie put the thought of him away. He would turn up. Or not. Whatever, they would manage.

Robbie was the only regular earner in the house and they scraped by on what he earned. His salt-selling job had gone with the rest of that industry. His new job as a delivery boy for a baker took him out of the Old Town, down below the Cowgate, toward the palace. It provided enough to pay the rent, but with very little left over for food. How much money there was for food and other essentials depended on how hard Robbie worked, and how generous he could persuade the customers to be. It helped when he had Essie with him, as he often did in the afternoons. Her smile could usually twist another coin from the toughest customer.

The baker, Mr. Brown, was a worried sweating smooth-cheeked man, almost entirely bald and shiny-headed. His hands and wrists were crisscrossed with ancient burns from the ovens and the girdle pans hanging over the fires in the back of the bakery. But he had never burnt a loaf or a pie or a plum cake in his life and his bannocks, his bridies and oatcakes were sought after across the whole of Edinburgh.

Robbie's job was to deliver the orders to houses, taverns and other shops or to fetch the supplies that Mr. Brown needed.

Robbie worked extra fast that morning. He made more deliveries in eight hours than he normally did in a day. By the time the two o'clock kail bell rang out from the steeple of St. Giles, he had done enough. At the bakery, he fixed a frown on his face as he spoke to Mr. Brown. "I'm awfy sorry, Mr. Brown,"—Robbie had long ago learnt to lose his educated accent when necessary—"it's ma wee sister. She's no' right, the day. Wuid ye mind if . . . ?"

"Och, awa' wi' ye. I'll see ye the morrow," and Mr. Brown waved a sweaty forearm in Robbie's direction. "I hope it's no' anything serious? Tha' wee Essie, she's a guid bairn." Everyone loved Essie. If there were a hundred hungry raggedy children, Essie's bird-bright eyes and crooked-toothed smile would shine out amongst their shadowed faces. She would never be left to starve. Her face was open and warm and her gaze was direct. People wanted to give her things—a cake, a pie, a pastry, anything to feed that smile. Most people did not see that she could bristle, too, and then her eyes were spiky, and her words sharp through her teeth, though she softened quickly. Her sparkle always returned.

"No, it's just a touch o' the cold, but ye ken how these things can change on a halfpenny. Thank ye, Mr. Brown, sir," and Robbie ran off.

Leaning into the biting wind, he walked up the hill toward their close. He bought a quarter of crusted cheese to add to the bread he already had from Mr. Brown.

Essie grinned, looking up from where she was roughly scraping out the grate.

She made a face at the food, but ate it hungrily enough anyway, tearing at the bread. One tooth was crooked, turning toward its neighbor, but all her teeth were strong and healthy, ivory in her stained face. After a while, she stood up, grabbing her shawl and wrapping it around her head and shoulders. She looked like a miniature grown-up. "Come on, Robbie. Let's go," she said. She liked to go with her brother in the afternoons and when their father was away Robbie liked to have her safe with him.

Robbie picked up his jacket and moved toward the door. "No, Essie, not today. I am not working this afternoon. There is something I have to do." He started to leave.

Essie followed him down the rickety wooden stairs and the final flight of stone steps out of the building. "If we had more money, Robbie, we could buy meat—mebbe a wee bit of beefsteak?"

"Food is all you think about! You are not coming with me." He felt gritty inside, the shrill wind needling him. A thin smurr, almost rain, wetted his face. By now they were through the tiny passageway onto the main street, Essie tagging behind.

"Please let me come."

"Stop whining!" snapped Robbie, moving faster. "I say you are not coming and there is nothing you can do about it." He had a bitter taste in his mouth. Essie looked stung.

Robbie stopped. "I am sorry, Essie. I have something to do. Something important. I will be back later."

Essie was still following him. "But—"

"Go home!" Robbie shouted, boiling over. There was a pause as they glared at each other, and then he watched his sister turn and run with furious legs back toward the door. He shouted, "Sorry, Essie!" but the anger was still too strident in his voice. A few people glanced over. The Highland porter at the corner, waiting in the cold with his sedan chair for a customer, looked at Robbie, then at Essie disappearing. His face was disapproving, and fierce with its huge orange beard. The porter, like everyone else, liked Essie, and he watched out for her where he would have ignored the other ragged children who ran wild through the streets. Robbie almost went after her, almost agreed to work a little more for some beefsteak for his sister. But she would come to no harm and he could wait no longer. Maybe he would bring her something later, to sweeten her again. He turned away, put her from his mind, and walked quickly toward Surgeons' Square.

Robbie did not know what he planned to do in Surgeons' Square. He just knew that if he ever wanted to find a way to make Dr. Knox know what he had done, he had to go there, to touch and perhaps enter the world of surgeons and knives and bodies. At the moment, he did not know how this might happen. He only knew it must.

Robbie found himself almost running. Twice he bumped into people. Once he was shouted at and someone started to chase after him, but thought better of it. There was something chilling in his face as he ran.

Usually he would have avoided the elegant thoroughfare of South Bridge, its new golden arches sweeping majestically over the midden of the Cowgate below. Usually he would keep to his familiar wynds and dank narrow side streets, but today he ran deliberately amongst the warmly clothed gentlemen along the gracious new road. Did he not have as much right as they to be there? Entering Infirmary Street from here, he ran straight toward the Infirmary and soon found himself, breathless, in Surgeons' Square. What now? He stood for a few moments, watching people coming and going. No one looked at him. The building where Knox had been the night before, and where the body had lain, stood tall and narrow in the left-hand corner, hiding its gruesome contents behind a gentle elegance. On the right-hand side of the square, he saw two men coming out of a severe building in the corner, their black coats thick against the February chill. Robbie waited till they had walked away. He moved toward this long, low building. The smurr had turned to sleet, slicing across his face. Ice on his eyelashes made him blink. He thrust his raw fingers deep into his pockets.

Surgeons' Hall, announced the carved stonework above the door. Another man was walking toward it. Robbie walked on but, as the man pushed the door open, he had a glimpse of marble, a huge roaring fire in a grate and something bright as silver, before the door closed.

"Clear off, boy!" Robbie leapt at the voice in his ear. He swung round. A man stood four feet from him, peering from underneath a large black object—an umbrella, the new fashion amongst Edinburgh gentry—his other hand holding a shiny-topped cane raised in readiness. Robbie stepped back. The man glared at Robbie through eyes set deep and steady in a high-domed forehead. His side-whiskers sprang sideways in a dirty gray froth. Above them his cheeks were red-veined from the cold and a drip gathered at the end of his nose.

Without thinking, and with his heart racing, Robbie blurted out, "Message, sir. For Dr. Knox." He was ready to run if necessary.

The man's face seemed to darken and his chin jutted forward. "Dr. Knox will no doubt be in his school." He sneered the last word. Robbie looked blank. "His anatomy school, boy. The building over there." He gestured with his cane toward the building where Robbie had seen the body the night before. He spoke mockingly, as though he wanted nothing to do with Knox or his anatomy school.

"Thank you, sir," said Robbie politely. He turned and walked firmly away toward Knox's building, his anatomy school, conscious of the man's eyes on his back as he went. Would the man wait to see if he went right into the building? But no, the man went toward Surgeons' Hall; the door opened and closed; and Robbie was alone in the square again.

He stood under the trees in the middle. What now? He looked at the clock high on a steeple lower down the hill. Half-past three. Still some daylight left. He did not feel satisfied. He burned with the need to act. He looked back toward Knox's anatomy school. How could he get in? And what did he hope to achieve? Yet he could not bring himself to leave.

He felt powerless in the shadows of these buildings. Of Surgeons' Hall, and Knox's anatomy school, and not far away the Infirmary where his mother had suffered at the surgeon's hands. At the thought, something ugly spat around his body. His armpits prickled.

In the gathering shadows and icy squalls, Robbie left the square and sheltered in a low doorway in the street outside, his muscles aching with cold. He could not go home. He waited. Watched the entrance into Surgeons' Square.

He did not have to wait long. Soon, the unmistakable profile of Dr. Robert Knox turned the corner and began to walk toward him out of Surgeons' Square. Knox was wrapped against the cold. He too had an umbrella to protect his clothes from the rain. How clumsy and strange an umbrella looked, thought Robbie. Knox's cravat sat high under his neck and a tall hat was set at a careful angle on his head. He stood for a moment, inhaling the air, the steam from a grating rising like hell-smoke around his feet, and then began to walk. Fast. He held a cane in the other hand and used it so forcefully that he seemed to be pulling the ground toward him as he strode.

He came straight toward Robbie.

Robbie's heart beat in his ears. His breathing quickened. As Knox passed by, the sweet smell of floral perfume drifted over him. Robbie held both hands over his mouth. Clenched his lips.

He forced his legs to move.

Robbie followed Knox at a distance. The gathering wind whipped his hair into his eyes. He did not care. He did not care about the freezing rain that spat over his face. Nor about the graying darkness and the fact that he was walking away from home.

He just walked, fast, keeping that tall frame in his view. Once on the main street, suddenly Knox stopped. Turned. Robbie stopped. Stooped and pretended to adjust his boot. Knox waved his cane at an approaching carriage. It clattered to a halt. Knox climbed in and the carriage rumbled off, with Robbie running after it. It was not hard to keep up— the wide street was crowded and the carriage had to swerve round people, other carriages, horses, barrows, dogs, pigs.

He must have followed it for half a mile or more before it turned into a side street and pulled up in front of a large-windowed house with shiny railings. Knox climbed out, easily, elegantly, paid the driver and went toward the house. It must be his house. Robbie had found where Dr. Knox lived. He watched the door swing wide and Dr. Knox enter.

Now, for the first time, Robbie began to feel the cold. His lungs hurt as he stood gasping in the icy mist. He stretched the collar of his jacket to cover his mouth, warming the air as he breathed it. The rough homespun material became moist. In this quiet, elegant street, Robbie became suddenly aware of his ragged, filthy appearance. His baggy trousers were torn at both knees, and too short, inches above his ankles. His jacket was also too small, with only one button left and the elbows threadbare. It smelt, he now realized, of ancient dirt and damp fires and meat grease. He wore his father's shirt, collarless, limp and filthy. His boots were mud-caked, dark with rain. Running his fingers through his hair, he tugged at the tangles. Suddenly, he could smell his own fresh sweat.

He walked through the gate, closing it silently behind him. Stepped softly up the flagstoned path. Winced at the gentle scrunch of his boots on the loose stones beside it. Slowly made his way toward the first window. Soon, he could see through the glass.

Inside, the room blazed with light. On the walls, fixed halfway up, were the glass globes that Robbie knew held gaslights. A fire burned in the grate. Robbie felt colder. Dominating the room was a huge dining table, set for ten or twelve people. Silver cutlery and delicate blue-and-white porcelain plates sat waiting. Cut-glass goblets, three for each place, sparkled under two enormous chandeliers, dripping with dangling crystal and holding too many white candles to count. Everywhere, jewels of light danced from reflecting surfaces, mirrors, silver and gold, as if someone had taken an armful of sunlight and thrown it high into the air.

A maid came into the room. Robbie shrank back a little but still watched. She fussed round the table, picking up pieces of cutlery and holding them to the light, adjusting glasses by a fraction.

There was another window a few yards along. Robbie

moved toward it, peered in. He saw it immediately. On a table in the window, an ochre-yellow violin, exposed, facing him, lying on its side. The bow next to it, carelessly laid, as though only recently left. Nearby, a music stand, facing the window. Robbie could almost see the composer's name. The notes looked complicated, flying over the page like insects.

Suddenly, a man walked into view. Picked up the violin and in one easy movement swung it to his shoulder. Knox! Robbie felt that rush again and his heart crashed.

At that very instant, Knox turned, for some invisible reason, toward the window. Robbie was frozen where he stood, as though pinned. For a stretched moment, Knox stared at Robbie and Robbie stared back. Then Robbie reacted, just as Knox did too. Knox dropped the violin, ran to the door of the room. Robbie stepped back, ready to run, and . . . screamed as a man gripped his shoulders with a shout.

Two men had been standing behind him. One now held him, lifting him by his shoulders. Robbie could not see them properly. The man's fingers dug into Robbie's flesh and his muscles would not work. Helplessly, he kicked his legs but his boots only brushed the ground.

At that moment the front door opened and Knox came out. When he saw Robbie dangling like a child, he laughed, leaning against the door frame.

"Well, well, well," he drawled. "What have you found, gentlemen? I confess I do not recall asking you to bring some entertainment to my *petite soirée.*" Knox's pitted face was creased with amusement, and his eyes, or his one seeing eye, stared directly at Robbie. Robbie burnt back, furious. He was too old to be held in the air. But the man who held him was much too strong.

"Peering in through your window, Knox, he was. Almost

had his grubby nose pressed against your clean glass," said the man who held Robbie.

"Been watching your maidservant, I should wager," said the other, his own voice wet with lust for the girl.

"Aye, well, bring him in, gentlemen. We shall see what the lad has to say for himself."

Robbie was dropped to the ground suddenly and pushed toward the door. He stumbled past Knox, who bowed slightly and clicked his heels together in mock respect. Robbie felt a sudden desire to lash out, to hit this evil, ugly man, but that would achieve nothing.

His thoughts scrambled as he was escorted across the hall and through a door at the end. The smells tumbled him back to a long-ago happier time—an oaky furniture smell, violin rosin, and . . . food! The unmistakable aroma of roasting pheasant brought him the memory of gravy ripe with plums and suddenly another memory, forgotten until now. His mother, hearing the clattering shout of the wine seller announcing a new arrival of claret in Leith, sending Robbie out onto the street to buy a jugful to taste. And him bringing it back, trying not to spill a drop, and his mother and father pouring themselves a glass and swirling it around so that through it the flames of the fire danced purple and warm. The memory now so vivid that it was almost unbearable.

Robbie now found himself in a room with a fire burning in the small grate and a comfortable chair to one side of it. One wall was covered from floor to ceiling in books. Another wall had panels painted pale green, with paintings of huge trees and scowling skies and temples. More gaslights on the walls, their steady flames clean. In the middle of the room sat a huge desk, its surface clear except for an inkwell and three knives. Each knife was slightly different. One had a thicker blade, fatter, fuller, swelling outward in the middle before tapering to a point. One was jagged, fierce, like a foxhound's teeth, but long, long and full of power. And the other was tiny, its blade no wider than a fingernail at its widest point, yet so sharp that its silvery edge slid invisibly into nothing. Robbie tore his eyes away.

There was the violin, lying on its back now. He stared at it. It had been in Knox's hands. Yet he wanted to touch its smoothness. Without thinking, he raised his hand and touched the side of his chin, the place where his own violin had used to rest. He realized that the men were watching him and he quickly looked away.

Knox was smiling, his dead eye fixed, his living eye bright and steady. He came toward him. Robbie stepped back. Nearer the desk. Nearer the knives.

"What were you doing, boy, staring into Dr. Knox's window?" It was the man who had held him, his bald head and narrow eyes giving him a cruel face.

Robbie did not answer.

All three men oozed wealth. Their shiny tailcoats gleamed in the firelight above their snow-bright breeches. Their hair was pomaded, the side-curls set perfectly, the smell of scent filling the air. Oriental designs swirled across their jeweled waistcoats, bright like peacocks.

But something still made Knox different from the others. There was something in the way he stood, in the way his jaw sat. He wore power like a cloak.

"Lost your tongue, have ye, boy?" This from the other man, smaller, shorter than Robbie, his head thrown back so that he could appear to look down his nose.

"Nothing."

"Nothing, *sir*," said the man.

"I believe the lad was observing my violin," said Knox.

"No doubt with a view to stealing it," sneered the bald man.

Knox spoke, his mellow voice hypnotic and soft. "Well, laddie, you have seen my violin. And now you see the owner of the violin. What do you have to say?" He stared down at Robbie, his lips lightly curled, his nose held high. Robbie stared back, though it took a huge effort to keep his eyes on that strange face. He fixed his gaze on Knox's seeing eye. Its hidden depths swirled, hazelnut and warm. Robbie was being drawn in. He tore his eyes away.

"What do you have to say?" repeated Knox, taking one step nearer and looming his face close. Just as he had done six years before, if he had only remembered.

"Nothing . . . sir," said Robbie. It was all he could say.

"Nothing? You have nothing to say to Dr. Knox?" snapped the smaller man, poison in his nasty little voice.

Knox spoke again, still watching Robbie, with a smile. "Aye, well, gentlemen, we are not inordinately interested in what the lad has to say, are we? Meanwhile, we have a dinner to enjoy, more guests to greet. What shall we do with this boy, eh? A puny specimen, do you not agree?"

Knox stretched a tapering soft finger toward Robbie. Robbie stepped back, toward the desk again. Knox moved more quickly and prodded him in the chest. "Puny, he is. No flesh on him at all." He laughed again.

Robbie's anger rose, boiled over, and in his fury, uncontrolled, he reached out and grabbed a knife, the one with the thicker swelling blade. But in the instant that he felt it in his hand, a numbing fear sliced through his body, and the knife dropped onto the floor. Knox leapt to pick it up. The small man snatched up the other two knives and held them away from Robbie. The other man rushed to grab Robbie, stretching his arms behind his back and locking them together by hooking one of his own arms through them. He forced Robbie's shoulders back brutally, almost paralyzing him.

He did not need to. As Knox approached, holding the glinting steel close to his face, Robbie felt the strength drain from him and he hung limp from the man's arm, eyes to the ground, his head swirling with faintness.

Knox held the blade to the light, breathed on it, wiped it on the lace of his cuff and held it to the light again.

"You chose well, laddie. This is a special knife. I designed it myself. It is not for delicate work. It is for . . . Look up, boy, look at the craftsmanship of this beautiful instrument." Robbie did not look up.

The small man shouted, "Look up, boy, when you are told." Still Robbie did not, could not look up. The man who was holding him gripped his hair and pulled his head back so that he had to look. He closed his eyes. "Open your eyes!" roared the small man. The large man twisted Robbie's hair until he had to open his eyes.

Knox continued. "Aye, as I was saying, laddie. A special knife, designed to slice through muscle, sinew, tendon, all in one go. Not so important on a dead body, where speed is not of the essence, but on a living patient, excellent, most excellent for slicing . . ."

He did not finish his sentence. Robbie had collapsed in a spiral of blackness, his shoulders wrenching backward as he fell forward, his legs rag-limp. The man let him fall and as he hit the ground he heard the three men laughing.

"Such a delicate constitution we often see amongst young ladies of the upper classes," said Knox. Shaking away the dizziness, Robbie pushed himself up onto his hands and knees and from there lurched to his feet. At the sight of Knox standing there, with the corners of his mouth turned up and open laughter in his face as his hand gestured courteously toward the door, every emotion Robbie had ever known was balled into purest rage. Their mocking farewells as he ran from the house were fuel to his anger. He stumbled down the steps, the door closing behind him. As he ran down the street, his fury grew.

At first as he ran, his anger had no words or order. It was pure emotion. And it felt red, blazing raw red. But slowly through the bloody mist burned the one clear thought: that Knox must suffer. If he had hated Knox before, now, now that he had faced him and felt his sneer, his hatred was a hundred times as strong. He could not rest until he had brought Knox down into the gutter with all the other filth.

Soon, exhausted, he slowed to a walk. He felt alone. There were still people on the streets, carriages, horses. But even so, he felt alone.

Walking past Infirmary Street again, he allowed himself to think of his mother's death. He had never felt alone before then.

He remembered kind women hugging Essie and the sickly lavender smell of them as they bustled into his house, gathering chubby Essie in their arms, with cries of "The puir wean." As for Robbie, he was told to "Be a man, now, Robbie." God had called his mother, they said. God wanted her. "Aye, the guid Lord gives and the guid Lord tak's awa'. And only the guid Lord kens the wa' o' it." Robbie's heart shrank under these words. They were meant as lessons of comfort and strength but for the first time in his life the words of the Bible did not seem to offer anything. A tiny sinful thought wormed its way into the crack in Robbie's heart: If God was so good, why would He take away a child's mother? The thought had frightened him. He hoped no one would see what was in his mind. He kept silent and his silence looked like strength.

Men would shake his hand and mutter emptiness. Robbie would look at his father, wanting him to say something to make everything right again, but it never happened. His father shut himself away, could not look properly into the eyes of his children, rejected the help offered by kind friends and relations. And after a while those friends and relations had stopped asking. Stopped calling at the close with a fresh bridie or a mill bannock or a fruit loaf wrapped in a clean cloth. Turned away by the silence and the emptiness and the sense of there being nothing they could do to help. "Pride comes afor' a fall," grumbled one wifie sourly as she left the house for the last time.

Mostly, Robbie remembered silence in his head. As though the world had stopped but would surely start up again at any moment. There were no words for what he felt and so he said nothing. As for Essie, she cried for a while but not for long. She never stopped playing with her kaleidoscope, though. She never tired of looking through the hole and trying to twist the toy to see the patterns change. "Scope, scope," she would demand, and Robbie would gently place his hands on her tiny ones and guide the sections round.

They did not move house. Robbie never quite knew why. Once, maybe a month after his mother died, he said something about "In our new house," but his father just looked at him, a desperate empty stare, then looked away, and said, "There is no new house." It just was not mentioned again. Robbie began to wonder if it had been a dream.

So for two years they had stayed, the three of them, in their old home, on the first floor of a building off the Canongate, a respectable place to live, not on the ground or top floors where the poorest people stayed. Still the stench and ugliness around them, but no more than anyone else had to bear, even people in well-paid work. They should have been satisfied. No servant lived with them, but a woman came each day to look after Essie and cook for them. Jeannie McKnight, she had been called, and they would never know how much they needed her until she was gone. Robbie carried on at school, learning his Latin and Greek and mathematics. His father wanted him to be a doctor. That was what had been planned for him from the very start, when his mother was alive.

"Study hard, my boy," said his father, his hand on Robbie's shoulder as he had struggled with his Latin composition one evening. "Study hard, and you will go to the university. You will be a doctor four years later. Think on that, Robbie. My son, a doctor! We shall be proud of you, your mother and I."

Robbie did not want to be a doctor. He would do it if he had to, but without his heart being in it. He wanted to play the violin. Wanted to play like Janiewicz. The chance of ever being as brilliant as Janiewicz was almost nonexistent, and earning a living as a concert violinist, without contacts or a rich patron to support him, would be next to impossible. But Robbie did not know this and such things meant nothing to him at that age. So, he could dream. He had not planned it or even spoken his dream aloud. To do that would be to destroy it.

He had only had a few violin lessons before his mother

died. The teacher, a tiny curled-up wiry man, whose back only straightened when he played the violin, his watery eyes white behind bent spectacles, had turned up for the usual lesson the very next day, when their home was dark with grief. He had left immediately, bowing out with his voice full of apologies in a thick German accent. Robbie remembered watching from a window as the man's coattails bobbed away round the corner, his white-stockinged legs picking their way carefully through the filth, his battered violin case held protectively under his arm and his back stooped under its own weight.

For two years, the three of them carried on. They lived almost as though things were just the same and the dreams had never been. The violin lessons started again. He learnt to curl his hand around the strings and slide his finger to find the exact note, and to sweep his bow arm smoothly across one string on its own, up or down according to the signs on the page. When he played, sending the highest squeaking notes swimming through the window toward the distant sky, he could float away with them and leave behind the ugly streets below. He could almost dream again. Could almost forget the empty space inside him, the place where his mother had left him.

Gradually, their father had begun to warm, to smile again when he came home from work with a present, to ruffle Robbie's hair or slap him on the back like a man or take Essie on his knee in front of the fire, jigging her up and down and quietly singing a nursery song:

"Come! Say your prayers, my bonnie bairn,
And saftly slip to bed—

Your guardian angel's waiting there,
To shield your bonnie head.

O never mind the foolish things
That clavering Robbie says . . ."

And here Robbie would join in, twisting silly faces at Essie to make her giggle.

"They're just the dregs o' ignorance,
The dreams o' darker days.

Our grannies, and our gran'dads too,
They might believe them a',
And keep themsel's in constant dread
O' things they never saw.

Lie still, lie still, my ain wee bairn,
Sic stories are na true,
There's naething in the dark can harm
My bonnie harmless doo."

And so things settled into some sort of life: kirk, lessons, their father's work, respectability. They began to live. Not to forget, but to move forward.

Then, two years after their mother had died, just when everything was turning toward something better, the fire. The fire that changed everything again. But Robbie would not think about that. Not now. Now he was nearly home and Essie would be waiting, especially if their father was not back. He quickened his step again.

In the High Street, almost at Fleshmarket Close, he drank

water from a well, scooping it from the bucket with his hands and throwing it over his face. Its peppermint coldness took his breath away.

Darkness had fallen already. Shadows scuttled around the tiny unlit cobbled streets of the Old Town. Stallholders had packed away their goods; shops had barred their entrances for the hours of darkness. Vegetable remnants and rotten scraps lay scattered. Robbie picked up some kail leaves and wiped the dirt off with his sleeve. A tavern door opened and two laughing men rolled out, followed by the warm breath of whisky. A woman, too, her tattered skirts hoisted high without shame as she slithered through the filth and stumbled in the doorway, shouting with laughter. The rain had stirred up the smells of human and animal waste.

In Fleshmarket Close, a ground-floor window was broken and, as Robbie walked past, a rat ran from it and slipped down the wall. Through the window he glimpsed a single candle casting its flimsy flicker over the exhausted scene inside. A baby weakly wailed, like a kitten in the darkness.

On the stairs he passed one of the women from the fourth floor. A Glasgow woman rented the room and had five other women as lodgers in it. The women shared two dresses between them. They took in sewing and knitted the feet in stockings to pay for their gin. Two of them would wear the dresses when they went to collect or return the sewing. The rest of the time they appeared only in incomplete underclothes or wrapped in a filthy blanket. At first, when Robbie and Essie and their father had moved to this building, they had been shocked by the women's lewd drunken hanging bodies falling out of their underclothes. Now, if Robbie stumbled across one on the stair, he hardly gave her a thought.

Robbie could see from Essie's face that their father was still not home. She had set food on the table and sat waiting, ignoring her own hunger. Her face flashed from fear to relief. Then anger.

"Where've you been?" her eyes blazed at him. He had no good answer. How could he have forgotten his sister? How could he have allowed himself to be drawn away from his home and into the world of Dr. Robert Knox?

He put the kail down, held his arms out, walked toward her, trying to warm her with his smile. He moved his hand to scruff her hair but she turned away, thistle-angry. She stabbed at the fire with a stick and it flared up, spitting.

"I'm sorry, Essie." Then he pointed to the table. "Look at this! A feast! Well done!"

She said no more as they sat down to eat, Robbie on the bed, Essie on a stool. The other stool empty. Robbie could see that beneath her anger, her clam-tight silence, had been real fear. It lingered in her eyes, and the streaks in the grime around them. It only fueled his guilt.

From the guilt, there was only a small step in Robbie's mind to the simple cause of all this. If Knox had not killed his mother, none of this would have been happening. They would be living comfortable lives in their new house, with time and energy to laugh and plan and dream. Food on the table each day without effort. Fresh air fluttering the curtains through the open windows in summer. A huge fire brightening their eyes in winter. Violin lessons.

"When will he come back, Robbie?" Essie stopped chewing as she waited for the answer, her mouth stuffed with bread.

"Oh, him. Who knows? I have given up wondering. We manage without him, don't we?"

"But what if *you* don' come back? What if you just don' come back one day? I thought . . . today . . ." Something swam in her eyes. She snapped her face away.

"Of course I will come back. How would I not come back?"

Essie looked back at him fiercely, her jaw clenched. "Promise me you won' go away. Even for one night." She managed to twist her fear into anger, as though she was ordering him instead of pleading.

"Of course I promise," said Robbie, believing it.

4

Thief

Next morning, Robbie woke even earlier than usual. His breath froze in the air above him. As he lay with icy feet under the coarse sheet and one thin blanket, his coat on top, waiting for the Cowgate clock to strike five o'clock, he thought of Dr. Knox. He burned with the need to act. Yet he seemed to have no power. What could he do to affect a man with the status of Robert Knox, with his wealth, his new house, his expensive clothes, his violin lying casually on its back?

He was still thinking about Knox as he made his way to the bakery in the frozen darkness of the early morning, slapping his hands together and stamping his feet to thaw them. Did Knox and gentry like him ever stop to think about the tired army of people who worked in the ice and rain and darkness to provide the food and services that kept their lives so comfortable?

His mind was not on his work that day. He was slow, unsmiling. Mr. Brown said nothing, but sweated more, pressed his lips together. Robbie missed one of the deliveries and found that it had been given to another boy, who grinned slyly at him. At lunchtime, when the kail-bell on St. Giles'

Cathedral rang out to mark two o'clock, he went home to get Essie, as he usually did when their father was absent. It was better if she was with him. And she was strong enough to be helpful. That afternoon, he and Essie traipsed from house to house with the bread barrow but earned little extra in the way of tips. Robbie's mind was elsewhere and Essie caught his mood.

They were hungry. Starved of energy. Their scalps were itchy, flaking. They had had no vegetables since a kail broth that Essie had burnt four days ago. No meat for longer. Breakfast had been oats mixed with water. Cold water. Fuel for the fire was precious—it took energy to collect and was usually wet.

Essie stopped. Her hand was pressed into her side, rubbing it. "I'm sore, Robbie. Can we no' stop?" She looked paler than usual, her skin tight over her cheekbones and some of the glimmer gone from her eyes. "An' my feet are soaked." She held out her foot and Robbie could see the sole of her shoe hanging off. He had cut a hole in the tips of the shoes some time ago, because her feet kept growing, and now her dirty toes glistened wet and red with cold.

He was suddenly irritated. He should not have to worry about her. His life ought not to be like his. He should be studying for university. Some boys of his age would be there already. He should not have to live from day to day thinking only about the next meal. He tried in vain to push his bitterness aside. Normally he simply did what had to be done and did not dwell on what might have been. But things were different now. His mind was being pulled in unusual ways. "Go home, Essie. I shall be back later."

"Why? Where're you going?"

"None of your business. I have to see someone."

"Who?"

"I told you—it's none of your business. Now go home."

"It's a girl!" She grinned, the hunger pains forgotten, her cheeks round again with laughter.

"It's not a girl."

" 'Tis so," and she started to flutter her eyelashes and pout her lips.

"Go *home*, Essie! Go away!" Taut with irritation, he kicked a stone and it hit an iron grating with a pistol twang. Heads turned.

Her face flinched into fury. "You're no' worth her, whoever she is." And she spun on her foot and ran away, the sole of her shoe splattering in the mud, her dirty skirts tangling in her legs.

Robbie put her from his mind. Essie would come to no harm. She could look after herself. Besides, she liked something to be angry about. He would make it up to her, buy a pie, bring her something. It never took much to smooth her feathers again.

Time to go.

He left the barrow behind some rubbish down a close where pigs grunted in a pen. The stink of a midden was ripe nearby. He would collect the barrow later and return with it to work as though he had never been away.

He set off for Surgeons' Square, choosing the familiar narrow streets. As he came closer, he walked more quickly. This time, he wanted to find his way inside one of the buildings. What did they do in there, those surgeons? Apart from cutting up dead bodies? What life did they lead inside those broad-windowed buildings? One thing was certain—it was not a life spent sharing a building with pigs, and rats crawling out of broken windows and gin-drowsy babies mewling before they died.

Past Infirmary Street he took a side street round to the back of Surgeons' Square and soon found himself behind Surgeons' Hall. He stopped, thought. How could he get in?

As he wondered, he saw two serving girls. He followed them toward the back entrance. The girls giggled and looked at each other as he nipped in front of them down the steps to the basement and held the door at the bottom open for them, bowing low with a smile as they went past him and through the door. But when he closed the door after them, he did not close it properly. After a minute to let them disappear, he pushed it open again and slipped in, unseen. He followed the dark mildewed corridor, its only light sifting through the tiny windows at ceiling level.

Round a corner, a door, locked. Another on his right. An open door ahead of him. Noise, light, laughter. The kitchen. Hot gravy smells. He slipped past. Another corner, a wider passageway, another door. Up some stairs and through a door at the top. The hall. Empty. Silent, huge. The smell of silver and an enormous crackling fire.

He stared up at the paintings high on the walls. Portraits of men, some seeming newly painted, the firelight leaping from their gilded frames. Serious-looking men with wise eyes and ruddy complexions, not smiling. Red or blue or black polished coats and shining white breeches with gold buttons. The light bounced from their cheeks, giving them a warmth that contrasted with their unsmiling eyes.

He heard footsteps. Quickly he hid in a doorway. A man walked across the end of a corridor, his head buried in a book, his coattails swinging.

Robbie took a corridor at the other end of the hall. He opened the first door, slightly. A fug of tobacco and a murmur of quietly talking men. He gently closed the door again.

The corridor turned to the left. He followed it. Three doors on each side of the corridor. All identical. All closed.

Silence. Though in the distance, when he listened carefully, he could hear the clattering sounds of servants, haphazard voices, wet wind on the windowpanes, a somber sleepy tick from the tall clock behind him. Footsteps. Far away.

Move. No point in standing there. Robbie opened the next door he came to, slowly, cautiously. Nobody. He walked in, looking round, checking each corner, casting his eyes quickly over each tall-backed chair. Nobody.

He was in a library. A smell he did not know, of oldness and difference. Something like tobacco but not. A sort of wood, perhaps. And stale air, trapped and heavy and still. Looking round, he saw, from floor to ceiling, row upon row of brown leather books. Most behind glass. In the middle, a table, covered with more books, some clothbound in the new fashion, and thinner publications. Journals. Robbie walked over, his feet squeaking loudly on the polished wooden floor. He picked a journal up. Its paper was thick, cream-white. It crackled as he turned the pages.

His eyes darted down the list of articles inside the front cover, haphazardly taking in titles. *Disease and the Poor. On the Methods of Elimination of the Small-Pox. Treatise on the Brain, the Eye, and the Ear. Excision or Amputation. New Principles of Surgery of the Hip Joint.*

He began to read, his mind entranced. It was difficult and he read slowly, stumbling, not understanding half of it. It contained strange words, many of which he struggled with, even with his knowledge of Greek and Latin, and it seemed to open up a new and frightening world. Diseases he had never heard of, ways of dying he had never dreamt about, operations he could not imagine. A world where people died and people lived, people suffered and were saved. Or not. Not his mother. Not at the hands of Dr. Knox.

Each time he read the chilling description of an operation with its cold explanation of gruesome techniques, his breath stuck in his throat and he wanted desperately not to read, but he could not stop. His eyes were dragged along the lines. His heart sped as the words took hold and he began to touch the edges of the minds of the men who had written them.

Nowhere did he find anything about the pain the patients suffered. Did these men not consider that? What was a doctor if he did not cure pain?

Was pain really God's will? Now that he was older, he began to hear the questions more clearly. But he was still afraid to consider the answers. What sort of a world was it where children were robbed of their mothers, and men and women were left screaming on a table, or dead, pinned open for anyone to peer into? Was there an easy answer? That it was God's will and he was not to ask why? Or was there another answer that would make better sense? Or was there no answer anywhere at all?

His thoughts returned to Dr. Knox. What had gone through the man's mind when he cut into Robbie's mother's flesh? Anything? The wish that she would stop screaming and let him concentrate? The hope that her blood would not spatter his lacy cuffs? And where was he now? Relaxing at home, smiling at guests, retelling the story of Robbie's fainting? Or at his anatomy school, his spindly fingers deep inside some misused body?

Robbie was just about to put the journal down, his skin cold, when the door suddenly opened. He spun round.

It was the man who had confronted him in the square. The one with the umbrella, the frothy sea gray whiskers and supercilious voice. And another, tall, ferret-eyed, bald-headed, with a tiny hard tight mouth that pinched itself together like an oyster. Both men, after a moment of surprise, moved quickly toward him, shouting for assistance. He had no time to run. They grabbed him, one at each arm. He was trapped. He would not demean himself by struggling.

The bald-headed man spoke, his thick cravat stuffing his collar full and giving him an air of bulldog strength.

"What have we here, Professor Syme? A thief?" His little mouth turned up, sneering.

"And a persistent one at that," agreed Professor Syme. "I have seen him before. Looking for Knox—for some ungodly reason, I've no doubt. This is not the first time you have been here, is it, boy? Running errands for the vile doctor. Stealing for Knox, were you?"

"I've stolen nothing, sir," replied Robbie.

"But what is this in your hand?"

"I wanted to read it."

Professor Syme's mouth twisted contemptuously. "Read it? What would you be doing with reading, boy? A liar, too. And not a good liar, at that."

"It is soap you should be looking to steal, boy," said the other man, his face creased with distaste.

By this time, two other men had come into the room and Robbie was surrounded. Men in tailcoats, exuding power, all large-seeming, puffed out by their layers of well-cut cloth, their necks thickened by cravats and tall collars. Everything he was not, in their uniforms of success.

There was nothing he could do. He held his head high.

"Take this filthy creature downstairs, Guthrie, and lock him up," barked Professor Syme. "Tell someone to get a constable. Fast. The boy is slippery."

With one arm twisted painfully high behind his back, Robbie was marched out of the room by two men. Across the hall, back through the door and down the same stairs he was pushed, as though they did not care one jot whether he fell and broke his neck.

He was thrust into a cellar, its wet air thick with mold. The key scraped in the lock, and he was in blackness. What now?

He did not have to wait long to find out. Within minutes, voices outside the door, the key turning again, and light flooding into the cellar. The man called Guthrie entered with two constables, one carrying a lantern, all stooping through the low door frame.

"Here he is," snarled Guthrie, unnecessarily.

"Thank ye, sir. We'll tak' him now. Turn ye'sen, boy." Robbie obeyed, turning his back to them. His hands were grabbed and he felt cold metal snapping round his wrists. Someone pushed his back and he stumbled out of the room.

On his way along the corridor toward the back door, he passed the serving girls whom he had met on his way in. They stared briefly, then turned aside with small frightened glances, before passing him. Robbie looked at the ground and felt himself blushing.

Outside in the lane, a black windowless carriage waited. He was pushed into it, as passing people stopped and stared.

Robbie sank into the darkness of a corner and shrank down inside himself.

As the carriage rattled its way over the cobbles, he could picture the passersby, stopping and trying to catch a glimpse of whoever was inside. He could see their shadows, like ghosts.

After a few minutes, the carriage came to a halt. A few seconds in the open air were enough to see where he was, even in the gathering darkness of the late afternoon. The Canongate Tollbooth's turrets pierced the scudding charcoal sky above them, its tiny windows black. Next to it, sharing a wall, the new tavern, its noise swelling through the open door. Once inside the Tollbooth, he was pushed along corridors, down worn stone stairs slippery with grease and dirt. He knew he needed to act. Ever since being caught, he had been paralyzed, powerless against all these stronger men. Now he had to do something.

He stopped. An angry curse came from the man behind him, and pain as a foot trod on his heel. He felt himself being pushed violently in the back. He stood his ground and turned.

"Please," he said, unable to stop the desperation in his voice. "I didn't do anything. Please just let me go. I didn't do anything!" His voice rose, spiraling with panic.

"It's no' my mess, gawkit laddie," replied the man, holding a lamp above his head. Nothing in his voice hinted that he cared. It was a cold voice, blank. "Git a move on, will ye?" And he pushed him again.

"I, I . . . if you let me go, I'll pay you," pleaded Robbie, not knowing what else he could say.

The man's eyes shriveled in contempt. "Pay me, wid ye? Aye, an' wi' what wid ye pay?" He hawked his lips together and spat straight into Robbie's face. The spittle ran down his cheek and over his mouth as his hands were freed and he was pushed into a cell. The tiny narrow door crashed shut behind him.

Robbie turned and beat the door with his fists until they hurt. "Let me out! Let me out!" he yelled, fear mixed with anger so that he could not tell which was which. But no one came, and he sank to the ground, pressed his forehead into the straw-covered floor and held himself until his heartbeat slowed.

Into the silence came a noise. A shuffling, grunting noise.

Robbie was not alone. He knelt up slowly, froze his breath, strained his eyes into the shadows. Something leapt at him from behind and he felt a cold hand, stinking and leathered, over his mouth. Another hand grabbed his hair and he was pushed facedown into the ground. His arms were squashed beneath him. He could not move. He could barely breathe, his mouth and nose pressed into the damp straw. The man, whoever it was, straddled his back and Robbie smelt his rancid breath and felt its warmth against his neck. A whisper, sibilant and wet, forced its way into his ear, "Hushie, pretty boy, or ye'll no' live tae tell the tale." And the man suddenly bit Robbie's earlobe. Something dribbled down his neck and he squeezed his eyes and mouth shut.

The hand moved from his mouth and he felt it creeping amongst his clothes. He whimpered through his nose. Into each pocket, through every cranny, between each thin layer squirmed the hand. The hand found what it was looking for, a coin, hidden deep in a pocket. Robbie had forgotten it was there. He could have bought food with it. Why had he not bought food with it, instead of letting it be found by this creature?

The man rolled away from Robbie and crawled on all fours

over to a corner. Robbie straightened up. He spat saliva from his mouth. And spat again to get rid of the taste, gagging.

He shuffled over to another corner as far from the man as possible, his eyes becoming used to the dark grayness of the cell. Sitting, wedged as deeply as he could into the corner, his knees bent up in front of him to shield his body, he fingered his earlobe where the man had bitten it. The cold wetness of the wall soaked into his back as Robbie watched the man.

He had never seen such a creature. A tangle of greasy hair fell over its face, so that it was hard to tell which way round the head was. The feet were bare and filthy, the toe joints thick like knots. The legs and arms were nothing more than bones, draped with sagging brown skin, hollowed. Then the man raised his head and the hair fell back to reveal a face. White eyes, round and wild. The mouth hanging open in a slack-jawed grin, as he held the coin up to stare at it closely. Four brown teeth at the front, like sticks. Suddenly laughing, the man threw his head back, wide-mouthed, and swallowed the coin. Robbie's heart stopped. Here was madness. This was how everything would end. He would surely die here and no one would know. Silently inside himself, a scream swelled and rose until he did not know how he could keep it in.

He slowed his breathing and tried to control his thoughts and calm his body.

The man half crawled, half stumbled away to another corner. Robbie watched him through partly closed eyes, wanting and yet not wanting to see what he did. He saw the man press his hands against the wall and move his face closer to the stone. The man's tongue hung out like a dog's and into the silence came the sound of the creature licking the wall, sucking up the mildewed water that ran in slow drips down the ancient stones. When he had drunk his fill, the man crumpled down onto the ground and curled up, muttering to himself in two voices. Occasionally he giggled.

Soon, the man seemed to sleep. Robbie had to stay awake. He tried not to think about the hunger that was eating at his stomach. Or the thirst. He tried not to think about what would happen to him tomorrow.

And Essie! What in God's name would Essie be thinking? Robbie could hardly bear to think of it.

What time was it? After dark, he knew. The cell had become almost completely black and Robbie realized that the earlier dim light had come from an encrusted grating at the very highest point of the cell, opening onto the street. Often, walking past this place, Robbie had heard the cries of grown men rising from the holes at boot level. He had always turned away and thought no more of whose voices they might be.

His sense of powerlessness was overwhelming. It rose in his chest and he screwed up his eyes against it. What have I done? What has Dr. Knox made me become?

Though Robbie did not sleep, his night passed in a torpid state somewhere between nightmare and reality. The cold was bone-deep. He tried to shrink as far into the corner as possible. He began not to feel bits of his body. A part of him was trying to stay awake, to plan how to escape and return to Essie. Another, stronger, part of him knew he could never escape. In this stinking hole, dying seemed completely possible.

At some time, during the darkest, most distant part of the night, the time when the heart slows almost to nothing, the time when death most easily worms its way into a sleeping soul, Robbie turned his face toward the wall and dragged his parched tongue against the dripping stones. And as he drank, he cried.

Afterward, he wrapped himself in his own arms again and

tried to rock his fears away. He strained his ears to hear the heartbeat sounds of his city. Everything was muffled by the thickness of the walls. Sometimes he stared at the grating, as though by seeing he could hear better. When he heard the sounds of the scavengers with their carts outside the grating, his face lit up and he tried to catch their words, desperate for any signs of the normal world. But he could make out nothing above the metal scraping of their spades as they shifted the filth of the streets.

He hunched down into himself again and drifted.

Eventually, the blackness through the grating began to soften into a dark grayness. Just as Robbie had decided that morning was approaching, the metal grate of bolts sliding and the lock turning jerked him into wakefulness. He squinted into the blinding glare of a lamp.

"Git up."

With difficulty, Robbie struggled to his feet. His body was cramped with cold and the sweat had frozen in his clothes. The other prisoner also lurched to his feet, grunting with excitement.

"No' you," growled the gaoler.

"How's tha'? No' me? When's ma turn, then? Eh?" The voice was cracked from lack of use. The prisoner moved toward Robbie and grabbed him by the arm. Robbie flinched. In the light of the oil lamp, he could see the scabbed face and desperate eyes.

"Get yer haunds off of him, scum. There's a mowbit breed for ye." The gaoler held out a loaf he was carrying, dangling it just out of reach of the prisoner, who leapt toward it with a cry. The gaoler threw it into the shadows of the cell and the prisoner fell on it, eating it like a wild animal.

"You. Oot," the gaoler said, gesturing with his head. Robbie did not need to be told twice. He left the cell.

"Go on—up the stairs," said the gaoler gruffly. "Ye're free to gae."

"How's that?" asked Robbie.

"A message came. Fae a genty doctor. Said there'd bin a mistake. Said ye should no' have been arrested."

Robbie's mind spun. "What was his name?"

"I dinnae ken. Aye, so I do. Knox. Dr. Knox, the message said. Must be a friend o' the magistrate. Ye've higher friends 'n ye shuid. Anyway, awa' wi' ye and dinnae ask questions."

Robbie left the building with his thoughts swirling. It did not make sense. Why would Dr. Knox do that? It could not be true. There must be some mistake.

Robbie would not, could never, feel grateful to Dr. Knox. No one wants to be grateful to an enemy. Either the gaoler had got the name wrong, or Dr. Knox had some evil intentions of his own, some new way to humiliate Robbie. Either way, it did nothing to Robbie's hatred of the man, except to fuel it further.

Now faint with hunger, Robbie hurried home. The city creaked into wakefulness in the almost darkness. A breeze, sharp and fresh, washed through his head. He put thoughts of Dr. Knox behind him and thought only of Essie. What would she be thinking? Would she be all right? He felt a sense of brewing panic as he climbed the familiar stairs, straining his ears for any sounds.

Even before he was through the door, Essie launched herself at him with an animal cry. She beat her fists against his chest. Robbie knew what he had done. He was the person who was meant to care for his sister, and he had not. He had left her, broken his promise.

He tried to grip her arms but she was strong. "Where've you been?" she shouted, staring up at him, ragged spirals of hair stuck to her face. Her eyes were red, exhausted. "You've been out all night. Where've you been?"

"I know. I am sorry. I just . . . I was . . . trapped."

"Trapped?"

Robbie walked to the other side of the room and stared out of the window, his eyes gritty with tiredness. Looking ahead through the grayness, all he could see were the lopsided roofs of other buildings, tumbling together, the gaps between them narrow and crooked like the wrinkles in ancient skin. But if he strained his eyes to the left, he could just make out, in the dark distance, the roofs of the New Town, a gentle glow from their streetlights. He turned back to Essie and told her exactly where he had been.

Essie's eyes opened wide. "But why'd you steal a book? We've too many books already."

"I did not steal it," snapped Robbie. "I was just looking at it."

"But what if you do it again? What if you get locked up again? An' what if they don' let you out and you go tae court an' then . . . what if you get hunged?"

"Hanged, not hunged," said Robbie, with a smile.

"Hanged, hunged, wha' ever!" shouted Essie.

"Because I won't," said Robbie.

"How d'you ken? Ye don' ken anything."

"Because I will look after you properly now. I've been foolish, Essie. I'm not going anywhere near that place again, and I will put Dr. Knox from my head. I will earn us money for food, good food, plenty of food, and I will study. I will go to university and then I shall have a good job to look after us properly."

"A doctor?" said Essie. "You was going tae be a doctor."

Robbie said nothing. What was the point in being a doctor? If God had ordered the world to include pain, how could he fight against that? No, the only sensible way was to earn some more money to improve their daily lives. Food, warmth, clothes and maybe one day a better place to live. Look no further than that and you will not be let down, he told himself. Even that might be a struggle, but it was worth it. He would throw off the madness of the last few days, walk away from the horror, concentrate on each day.

As he thought it, he could almost believe it. Even thinking it made him feel lighter.

Essie needed him. Not that she would admit it. They needed each other. When she was not helping him, she worked hard herself, doing what she could to help them survive. Often she earned money running errands for the stallholders at the flesh market, or the many other traders who propped their stalls wherever they could.

When he returned in the evenings, Essie would have queued for water from the public well, carrying it in several journeys up the stairs to the fifth floor, her face red with exertion and sweat streaking the dirt on her cheeks. Occasionally, she might have washed some clothes or their sheet, treading them with her feet in cold grayly sudded water. She would have found firewood to add to the pile they tried to keep constantly drying by the fire, or coal if she was lucky and if her pockets had room in them. She would have collected tinder, scraps of dead grass or sticks or even paper, and she would gather it in her pockets and fill their tinderbox with it, leaving it by the fire to dry. If they ran out of tinder, they had nothing with which to start a fire in the evening, and then the cold would settle in their bones overnight and by the morning their sheet would be iced over with frozen breath. The water in their jug would be frozen thick.

She might have picked up some food from the ground by the market stalls, anything from kail leaves or a turnip to a scrawny pig rib or fallen piece of oxtail from the flesh market. She was quick like that, and her pockets were deep. Her smile, though not innocent, was clear. No one could resist her fire-bright eyes. Robbie could imagine that if someone caught her thieving, the victim would not call the authorities but would pat her on the head and even give her an extra coin for her daring. Each evening when Robbie came home she would proudly produce what she had won that day—perhaps an apple, or even some cheese. Once a whole portion of beefsteak, suspiciously clean and undamaged.

Each evening, though exhausted, he would still find time to teach Essie her reading. She would scowl and fidget. "What's the point, Robbie?" she would mutter, twisting her fingers around each other as she struggled to read the long words he gave her.

"The point is so that you can read the Bible," Robbie would say.

"I ken what the Bible says. Mr. Chalmers reads it tae us."

Recently, Essie had started at Sunday School. It was her own idea. She had stood at the door one day and watched the shiny rows of children happy all together. She'd shouted out the answer to an arithmetic question and the startled teacher, a young wispy man with a weak voice and long fluttering hands, had invited her in. She loved answering the questions more quickly than anyone else, and then running away at the end before the teacher could catch her to ask more about her family circumstances. She had lied already. Dead mother— well, that was true enough—dead father, no brothers or sisters, lived with an aunt and uncle, went to school every day of course, sir . . .

She liked it because it was different from every other day of the week. It did not hurt her hands or make her hungry. There was something sure about it. Something warm and routine. And there was something to eat at the end of it too, quickly snatched before she ran off.

"Why do I have tae read the Bible? I ken what it says," she would repeat to Robbie.

"It's right, Essie. It's just right," he said, wearily, not thinking below the skin of the words.

She would just look at him, and her eyes would seem to know more than she was saying. He would turn his eyes away and she would carry on reading, her voice dull. And he would wonder, too, what the point of it was. But one day there just might be a point. If you did not think that, what would you do?

Robbie wished Essie would go to school properly. There was a free school, but it was run by the kirk and they did not belong to a kirk. Besides, their father would not consider asking for charity from the kirk, even if they had belonged. He had heard ministers preach against poverty often enough—it was a punishment from God, they said. He was not blinded or crippled by ill fortune, so he was not one of their so-called "deserving poor."

Sunday School and Robbie's teaching. It was not much, but it would have to do. He must hold on to the idea that there was a point to it all. But it was hard to hold on to, what with the endless daily task of finding food and warmth. Keeping their heads above the pig-swill streets.

Now, his heart lifted as he saw the fire in Essie, that surviving spirit in her coal-bright eyes. He needed her spark.

76

A curl of black hair spiraled over one of her eyes. He moved his hand to brush it aside and she scowled but let him do it anyway.

Together they ate an oatmeal and water brose. Robbie stopped suddenly, dropping his spoon. His hand went to his forehead and he swore. "Hell's fire! The barrow! Quick, Essie!" He had left the bread barrow the evening before and had never returned to the baker's shop with it. Surely it would be stolen by now, or swept away with the rubbish by the scavengers whose job was to clean the streets at night.

"Come with me, Essie! Hurry!" He threw her shawl toward her, grabbed his jacket. They pulled on their shoes and boots and together they ran down the stairs and out into the sleepy charcoal morning. They sped through the early-morning crowds, Essie not knowing exactly what it was they were running for. Robbie ran fast, his feet thumping out his prayer, "Let it be there! Let it be there! Let it be there!" His tongue was dry in his mouth. He would lose his job, surely, if it was gone. Even Mr. Brown, tolerant as he was, would never let him get away with that. But with Essie beside him, there was a chance Mr. Brown would not be too harsh.

Into the narrow close, round the corner, past a man lying curled against a wall, vomit and blood around his head. Past the midden, and the one privy that served several streets, its low door swinging wide, the pit overflowing. There were the pigs, their snouts buried in rotten turnips. There was the pile of rubbish. No scavengers that night, then. Where . . . ? There it was! There was the barrow. Robbie could have sung aloud. Everything was going to be all right. This was a sign. From now on, God was on his side.

The barrow was filthy. It had been underneath a window and someone had thrown the contents of a chamber pot onto it rather than use the midden. They cleaned it as best they could with grass grabbed from the edge of the Royal Park, and hurried to the baker's shop.

Mr. Brown's sweaty face greeted them, frowning, flustered. "How d'ye explain ye'sen, laddie? Where did ye go yesterday?" he spluttered. His hands were on his wide hips, his fingers splayed, dough sticking to them like tatters of flesh. Essie smiled sweetly up at him and he reddened, his lips melting. She spoke, falling into a broader Scots accent as she widened her eyes to him. "Sorry, Mr. Brown. It wis ma faut. I wis no' weel, ye ken, an' Robbie had tae look after me. But I'm a' better. An' I'll help ye all the week long, I will so." For a moment, Mr. Brown simply stood there. Then he softened. There was nothing he could say. He could no more have been cross with Essie than he could have stamped on a blackbird's egg. He was under her spell like everyone else. Mr. Brown helped them load the bread onto the barrow, and gave Essie a piece of gingerbread with a sugar rose on it. Her cheeks crinkled as she bit into it. She looked at Robbie and gave him a secret smile.

A weak filtered sun began to whitewash the past few days as they set off on their deliveries.

God was on their side at last, thought Robbie.

5

The Resurrection Men

It was now the beginning of March, and each day grew lighter, brighter as the waking sun trickled its warming fingers across the city. Often, still, the chill wind whipped itself up and the icy rain dripped down bare necks, but these were the final weapons of winter. Now, bulbs began to spray their colors across the grassy spaces. A few fresh vegetables appeared in the haphazard filthy stalls that sprung up like weeds in the shadowed archways. Girls sold daffodils, their cheeks rose-red, their hair floating free, blown like meadow grasses. Spirits lifted.

Robbie threw himself into rebuilding their lives. Each day he worked hard, often with Essie at his side. They earned enough to buy Essie shoes. She leapt around their room, delighted with the stiffness of the new leather, her blackberry curls bouncing past her shoulders now. That day, they had a rabbit, broiled in the broth pot until the flesh dropped away from the bones and the flavor caramelized.

Robbie threw himself into his studying, reopened the schoolbooks that were piled under the bed. Books were among the few possessions their father had not sold. He thought they were either not worth enough, or worth too much.

Robbie kept Essie at her studies, too, though this was a struggle. She could not see the point, but if it meant she had food at the end of it she would do it. She was bright, quick to learn. Sometimes, though, when Robbie looked at her filthy clothes, ragged black fingers and nut-brown face, he wondered how she would ever marry. It was her childlike spirit that drew everyone to her, but what would she be like when she was no longer a child? There was nothing of their mother in her. Essie was all fire and thorns, thistle-sharp and magpie-bright. She had none of their mother's fragile poppy lightness.

He loved Essie. Not that he would ever tell her so. He did not imagine she ever thought of things like that. She was too caught up in living. And she did live, too—much more than survive. Essie threw herself at life, her sparkle darting, too fast to catch.

So, for this short time, their world was steady, warm, solid.

Until the tide changed. It happened late one evening toward the end of March. The darkness was still that night and gentle for the time of year, the cold wind resting. Essie was at home before Robbie that evening, making the fire, preparing their meal. Robbie had delivered a load of special Easter breads to a large house at the foot of Arthur's Seat and had returned the barrow to Mr. Brown. Mr. Brown had given Robbie a simnel cake. "Fae Essie. Put a wee bittie color in her cheeks." And he smiled as he wiped his forehead.

Robbie lingered outside for a moment in the fresh air as it washed off the hillside, bringing the scent of pines and the sea. A faint whiff of gunpowder from the tunnel blasting. He kicked a stone idly and ran to follow it as it bounced haphazardly, skittering across the rough cobbles. Suddenly, he felt an overwhelming urge to go home quickly, to join Essie and bury himself in his books again.

He began to run, soon coming to the buildings that edged the Royal Park, large mixed with small, the smells of burning metal from a smithy mixed with sweeter toasted smoke from the brewery. Across the main street, up the Cowgate with its buildings tottering above his head. He wanted to get home. He took a shortcut, running up a steep dark alley, dodging the rubbish piled against the walls, the sewage in the gutters. A shout from above but, before he could move, a bucket of filth sloshed just behind him, its stinking contents splashing his trousers. Leaping aside, he rounded a corner too fast. Coming toward him were two men pulling a cart. There was something jumpy, something secret, about their actions, and Robbie slipped into a doorway, intending to hide until they were past.

The cart had almost come level with his hiding place, when one wheel hit a stone and spun off-center, tipping the load onto the ground. Both men cursed, and ran to the cart, looking around them. Both had squashed, misshapen hats pulled down over their eyes and the collars of their baggy coats turned up. One held a lantern with a tiny guttering flame. He put it on the ground. They crouched over the fallen load. It was a large barrel. One of the metal strips around it had slipped and two of the laths had sprung away. The ropes that had tied it to the cart hung slackly. The cart leaned at a useless angle.

Robbie gasped, and slapped his hands to his mouth to silence his own noise. He could hardly believe what he saw. Through the broken laths of the barrel, an arm, a human

81

arm, hung, swinging stiffly like a broken pendulum, its fingers clawed.

One of the men stuffed the arm back inside and tried to push the slats roughly back into place, sliding the metal strip downward. Together they hauled the barrel upright and as they did so the lid sprang off. Robbie held his breath, his thoughts racing. But it was the words he heard them speak that sent his heart spinning crazily and all the strength washing from his legs.

The words flew clear as glass, the rolling Irish accents shattering the sheltered silence of the alley, smashing any traces of the peace that Robbie had conjured during the last days.

"Mary Modder of Jesus! Knox'll no' be pleased, an' he won't. Wid ye look at that?"

"For sure and how'll he pay us a full price for that?" muttered the other man more quietly.

"Bastard! Never needs an excuse to rob us. And look, wid ye—head smashed. Bastard'll never pay up now." The voice was snarling, low, as the man looked inside the damaged barrel.

The first man spun round. Then the other. They had both heard it: a gasp from the darkened doorway. The first man ran over to where Robbie was hiding. A knife glinted in a hand. He grabbed Robbie's jacket and dragged him out, peering at him in the shadows. Robbie could not see where the knife was.

The man pushed his face close to Robbie. He was chewing dried fish and the stink of it swam from him. The second man leapt round and both of them pushed Robbie backward to the ground, his body pressed over the barrel. Robbie's head was inches from the smashed human contents.

The first man held him by the throat with one hand, the knife in the other, held so that its cold edge pressed into the skin lower down on Robbie's neck. Dark-ringed eyes inches from Robbie's. Tiny red veins across the sticky-rimmed eyeballs. One eye larger than the other, and higher. Beads of sweat springing from a thin face iron-black with bristle. And scars, twisted across his forehead.

"What have we here?" The man's full red lips were spittled. He chewed slowly on his fish, making a sticky sound. Through the open wet mouth protruded two front teeth, unusually huge, and crossed. It made him look like a rat, with a mouth that could never quite close. The knife rested against Robbie's neck. He could hardly breathe.

The second man spoke, his voice softer, smoother, his pale eyes narrowed so that the near-white lashes almost hid their rabbit pinkness. His pale skin was covered in light brown patches, freckles merged into each other like pools of wet sand. "Wid ye get rid of him, William? We've no time for gabbing. Kill him quickly and quietly, afore he gets us killt."

Robbie struggled to speak, his voice squeezed. "Please let me go. I won't say anything. I have a sister to look after."

"Sister, eh? Pretty as you, is she?" The scarred man's wet lips turned up into a smile.

"Get rid of him, William. We can't keep the good doctor waitin', for sure. The boy is not'ing to us, but Knox is our wages." The pale eyes were looking down the street, wary. Briefly, the moon appeared and shone through the thin hair wisping from under his squashed hat. His neck was tree-trunk thick, but his body and limbs were thin and skin-lagged.

Someone came round the corner but doubled back and walked away quickly. No one was going to help Robbie.

"Could be anodder body to sell. And sure, such a fresh

83

young body at that. Not a mark on it, will ye look at it?" It was the rat-toothed man who spoke, greedily.

The other man looked at Robbie and was silent for a moment, thinking. Robbie knew they could kill him easily. Even apart from their strength and his helplessness as he lay forced over the broken barrel, the knife edge against his neck left him paralyzed. He could not even turn his face from the spittle and open lips and foul fish breath. From their leering faces he knew they would do it as happily as they would kill a rat.

"I won't talk. I can help you. I . . . I know Dr. Knox. I've seen where he works." He had no plan. He just said it to show that he had some weapon, that he was not just any boy. He said it to make them pause. They froze. Then the one with the knife drew his face closer and the knife pressed harder until Robbie thought it must break his skin.

In a whisper as smooth and quiet as blood, the sandy-haired man spoke softly, bringing his mouth close to Robbie's ear, the sick-sweet breath warm over his face.

"So? You know Dr. Knox? Friend of his, we're thinking? What would the so-clever Dr. Knox be doing wit' a friend like you?"

"No, not a friend. I hate him!" The one holding Robbie loosened his grip. They both studied him more closely, their eyes narrowing. Then they stood up straight, and let go of him, though they stayed close. Watching him. Thinking. But slowly. He breathed, dared to move his hand to touch his throat.

Robbie could perhaps have made his move then. Could have leapt to his feet and run away and put them behind him. Could have returned to Essie, to his sensible hardworking life. But once more he had come across that name. Dr. Knox. He could not turn away.

Suddenly, he realized exactly what Dr. Knox had to do with these men. Robbie knew who they were. Not their names. But what they were. Resurrection Men. Everyone had heard about, and learned to fear, the Resurrection Men. Men who robbed new unguarded graves at night and then sold the bodies. And who bought these stolen corpses? Surgeons. To cut up and explore the workings of the human body. Surgeons like Dr. Knox. The law allowed them only the body of one hanged criminal a year, Robbie remembered hearing, but one body was not nearly enough for some of them—men like Dr. Knox.

So, this was how Dr. Knox found the material for his evil hobby. This was how he practiced, on stolen bodies, as well as on the living. Robbie's head spun. Dr. Knox paid these men, he said to himself. How apt if Dr. Knox were to pay him, too. Here was a way to enter Dr. Knox's life and, this time, Robbie would not be the victim.

"I can help you," he said quickly, rubbing his throat. "You need me. I can help you pull the cart, or I could be your lookout. I'm fast." He scrambled to his feet, and saw out of the corner of his eye the smashed head squashed inside the barrel, twisted at its neck to make it fit. The stench of fish and the sea swept across Robbie's face. It was a herring barrel, he realized, its sides slimy with silver scales.

The man with the sandy hair and pale-lidded eyes spoke, in little more than a whisper, taking one step closer again.

"See that body? You set one step out o' line, you so much as whisper a word o' what you've seen, and the next body will be you, so it will. And your friend, your friend what you say you hate, he'll be the one to cut you up, to slice off the skin from your legs, to open up yer gizzard like a herring, to lift out yer eyeballs one by one and pin t'em to a table. We seen it done, boy, and we'll see it done to you, sure we will." The words oozed slow and sinister as blood.

Robbie somehow stood his ground. "I won't talk," he promised, his voice no more than a breath.

"Now, be getting that wheel on," continued the man. Both men leaned all their weight against the cart while Robbie positioned the wheel and slid the bolt through. The scarred man spun it fast a few times. It wobbled but it would do. The pale man forced the lid back into the mouth of the barrel and then the three of them lifted it back onto the cart, tying it down as firmly as they could with the ropes.

The two men looked at Robbie, then at each other. The scar-faced one raised a hand and passed the knife across his own throat in a slitting motion. "No," cautioned the other man quietly but firmly. " 'Tis better this way, so 'tis."

His companion looked at Robbie and made the same throat-cutting motion again, slowly. "One step out o' line, boy, an' you'll go the way of the horse. We had a horse what pulled the cart, did we not? But the bastard horse had no stomach for pulling dead bodies and it would not move. An' we killt the bastard horse, so we did, shot it through the eyes wit' a pistol. One step out o' line, boy . . ." and he spat the gob of fish onto the ground at Robbie's feet and wiped his lips with his hand.

The pale man laid a large freckled hand on his companion's shoulder and spoke to Robbie, his hard eyes penetrating. "Knox's place, boy. On wit' you." The man picked up the lantern and they set off, Robbie running ahead, peering round corners and checking for constables or bailies

86

or soldiers before beckoning to the men to follow with the cart. He did not think about what the cart was carrying. Or of Essie waiting at home. He thought of nothing but Dr. Knox and as he did, the anger burned. Excitement, too. Now he was doing something.

As Robbie turned into the steep hill leading to Infirmary Street, he heard a whistle. He looked round. The two men were in the shadows, gesturing to him. "Not up dair, eejit. The back," urged the sandy-haired one. Robbie was confused. This was the way to Knox's anatomy school, was it not?

The other man snapped, his voice spittled with tension, "Mary, Modder of Jesus, wid ye jist get a move on? Down there, round the corner and in the Flodden Wall . . ." but before he had time to finish, Robbie spotted the tall figures of two constables. Coming their way.

"Move! This way!" His voice so urgent that the men did not question him. He grabbed the cart himself, hauled it with them up the steep slope. Quickly to the left, into the small courtyard of a building. In the shadows. Silent except for breathing. Robbie squashed against the barrel. Trying not to smell it. The three of them. Mingled sweat stench of bodies too close together. Fish whisky breath. Wide eyes. Fixed on each other. Not daring to move. Or look into the street. Footsteps. Approaching. A sudden crunch as the cart shifted, settling. Do not breathe. Go away. Go away. Go away. Please God, go away. Going away. They breathed again. Wild-faced, the two men began to move. "No, wait," said Robbie. He moved out of the courtyard, down the slope, and cautiously peered into the main street again. The danger had passed. They had not been seen.

The sandy-haired man clapped Robbie on the back, his hand powerful despite his small size. Robbie would not like to fight a man with such hidden strength. "Good work, lad, to be sure." The other man wiped his wet mouth with a sleeve and held out a hand to Robbie. Reluctantly, but with a strange excitement, even pride, Robbie took his hand and felt its limp bony coldness as he shook it. The man smiled, those teeth like crooked gravestones in the glow of the lantern. When he smiled, his lopsided eyes remained dead, brackish, the smaller one closing further, the larger one remaining open, watching.

They all moved off again, Robbie in the lead. The Flodden Wall towered above them, its ancient stones thick and strong. Where now? The two men gestured to Robbie to wait on the other side of the road, out of sight. He stood pressed against the side of a building and watched.

There was a doorway, low and dark, set deep into the wall. Robbie had never noticed it before. He looked up. Above the wall rose a tall narrow building . . . and then he realized. This was the back of Knox's anatomy school. After looking round to make sure no one was approaching, one of the men knocked on the door. A moment later, it opened and Dr. Knox himself came out, looked around. Robbie's heart began to race. The dark-haired man used his knife to prize the lid away from the barrel. Dr. Knox looked inside it, poking the contents with his fingers. The conversation became angry. The two men began to replace the lid and move away with the barrel still on the cart. Dr. Knox followed them. Robbie could see his face, yellow under a nearby gaslight, pitted like curds. Some more words and Knox pulled something from his pocket. He began counting money into one of the men's hands.

The man held his hand out for Knox to shake, but Knox turned away with a casual gesture of his arm, his lacy wrist turning with swanlike grace, his tapering fingers softly curled as if playing a violin. Two more men came out, young men, perhaps students, and hefted the barrel off the cart before rolling it carefully indoors. Knox followed. The door closed firmly.

Robbie walked over to the men, who were crowing over the money they had been paid. Robbie had never seen so much money at one time.

"More t'an ever, stupid bastard!" The man's pale eyes gleamed as he handed money to the other one.

"Easy money! Bee-oootifully easy money," laughed the wet-lipped one, his tongue sticking out as he counted his share. Robbie stared at it.

"Want some, boy, d'ye? What d'ye tink, William? Will we be generous?" the pale-haired man seemed relaxed now, louder, buoyed up by their success.

"Sure, we can afford to be generous, William. And anyways, he needs feeding, so he does. Skinny as a rat, he is. Push the cart, boy, and ye'll get yer pay when we get home."

Robbie pushed the cart the whole way back, lighter now with just rope for its load, through the Grassmarket and into West Port, the two men leading the way in high spirits. They came to a stop outside a crumpled inn. The door opened and a wave of noise and light and warmth spilled onto the cobbles. A woman came out as soon as she saw them, shouting at the two men.

"Where've ye bin, ye lousy bastards? What took ye so long?" But she was smiling, her lips wide and loose.

"Trouble wit' de cart. The lad helped."

The woman peered at Robbie. From her dress, Robbie had at first thought that she was young, but her skin was mapped with broken veins and her hair, uncovered, was gray and dry. Her cheeks were streaked with vermilion, carelessly applied. Her low-cut dress revealed her upper chest and throat, its skin wrinkled like a dirty sheet. Her bodice had slipped sideways, exposing more of one breast than the other, but she did not notice. Lurching slightly, she moved too close to Robbie, stretching her eyes wide as she struggled to focus on him. She reeked of used sweat.

"We have money, Margaret. Would ye look at this? An' the boy needs a drink, so he does." The rat-toothed man flung his arms round the woman, who grinned slackly. Before Robbie could stop them, he had been swept into the tavern. Inside, all was noise and steam, bodies and confusion. A swollen roar of voices. The smell of roasting meat. A warm fug enveloped him.

Someone thrust a lidded pewter tankard into his hand. He looked around. Faces, shouting, laughing faces everywhere. He did not know where to go, what to say, whom to look at. He caught the eye of a girl across the room. She stared straight back at him, long black curls spiraling over her eyes, pink roses on her cheeks, and opened her little red mouth, sticking her tongue between its lips suggestively. He blushed and lifted the tankard's lid with his thumb before burying his face in the ale. He had had ale before but this was more bitter, stronger, darker. He drank more, felt its warm strength gushing through him, welcoming.

He leaned against the wall, his head against the stone, and let the noise wash over him. He drank again. The warmth was in his stomach now, spreading outward. He watched the swarming faces until they all merged together. It seemed as though everyone was laughing, heads thrown back, mouths gaping. Voices became louder and louder, each competing to be heard.

There was something comforting about so much laughter. Robbie began to smile too. He closed his eyes and just bathed himself in the warm chaos around him. He need do nothing, think nothing, just close his eyes and relax while the voices ebbed and flowed around him.

Suddenly he felt a hand on his arm. He opened his eyes. It was the darker of the two men. He smiled through spittle-lips, and swung one arm round Robbie's shoulders as he spoke, his voice softened by drink.

"Wha's yer name, boy?"

"Robbie."

"Well, Robbie, how'd ye like to work for us again? Next time we have a . . . delivery, for your friend—sorry, not friend—Dr. Knox? There's good money in it, so there is."

Why not? It was, as the man said, good money, and easy work. Surely Dr. Knox owed them, Robbie and Essie, for what he had done?

"Aye," said Robbie. "Where will I come? And when?"

" 'S not reg'lar work. Come here every day, after dark, and we'll tell ye if there's work, so we will. Ask at t' door for us."

"Wha's your names?" slurred Robbie.

"William Hare, at your service," replied the man, his hand to his scar-twisted forehead in a mock salute. When he smiled, his black eyes gleamed and his wet lips curled out to reveal their shiny pink insides. "And my quieter friend is William Burke."

Hare fumbled in his pocket. Bringing out a handful of coins, he pressed four into Robbie's hand. Robbie stared at them. He closed his fingers round them and felt their solid metalness. This was more than he would earn in a week at Mr. Brown's. Even with tips and Essie's smiling face.

Hare then shifted his face closer to Robbie's. In the hazy distance, Robbie could see Burke walking toward them, pushing his way across the room. Before he arrived, Hare's black eyes drilled into Robbie's. "Now listen. And listen good, boy. Now ye've been paid, ye'll no' talk. Ye're in this with us and if ye talk ye'll hang with us, I swear to the good Lord, so you will. We hang, you hang."

Before Robbie had time to think, Burke was with them, pressing one of three small thick pottery cups toward Robbie. Robbie put his tankard, now empty, on the ground and took this new drink. Burke gave another to Hare, leaving one for himself. "Here's to us, my friends," he said, raising it and looking straight at Robbie, his pale eyes watering in the smoky air. They were thinking eyes, without emotion.

"And to the good doctor, to be sure," added Hare. "May he continue to need our work for a long time to come. Drink up, Robbie boy." Robbie looked for a short moment into the whisky. As he drained it back, an image of his father came unwanted into his mind, but the burning liquid drowned all such thoughts as the fire hit his stomach. For a few seconds he could not breathe or swallow, but soon his face emptied into a grin and the blood spun through his body, giving him a strength he had never felt before.

Later that night, much later, he stumbled dizzily up the stairs to his room. Two of the sewing women sat on the stair, one puffing on the pipe that stuck from her mouth, both slack-jawed with gin. They swayed toward him with a lewd laugh. His reactions were slow and he felt his leg grabbed. Angrily, he kicked his foot from their grasp and stumbled up the stairs, followed by their wheezing laughter.

In his room, he could remember little about anything that had happened in the inn, except the warmth, the money in his pocket, and the fiery strength the whisky had given him.

As he fell fully clothed into their bed, only stopping to kick off his boots, he did not notice that Essie was still awake. He did not notice her lying there like ice.

6

Sliding

Robbie woke early with a stagnant mouth. His head throbbed sickeningly as he sat up, his eyes hot and metallic. He fumbled to light a candle from the orange glow of the ashes and the damp wick fizzled before it lit. His urine was dark, the stream seeming to go on forever. Steam rose from the chamber pot into the icy air.

He shuffled back to bed. The next thing he knew, Essie was shaking him.

"Get up, Robbie." She shook him again. "It's morning and it's the Sabbath."

"Go 'way." He did not want to speak. Every word tasted foul. He could smell his own breath.

Essie pulled her clothes on quickly, her fingers fumbling in the cold. Kneeling by the fire, she blew gently on the embers, feeding them tinder and then larger sticks until they burst into flame. She picked up the jug of water and poured some into the broth pot, which she hung from the grease-caked hook above the fire. They had no kettle anymore—when the old one had a hole in the bottom, Robbie had taken it to the blacksmith, but the blacksmith, instead of repairing it, had offered him money for it. He would melt it down and make horseshoes. Robbie had taken the money, though it was little enough. So now they boiled water in the broth pot and all their food tasted of old grease and kail. Essie mixed oatmeal into the warmed water, stirring the thin brose with a cracked spurtle. She ate in silence, quickly.

She watched Robbie, strangely wary of him. A tiny splinter of something almost like fear pressed against the fragile skin of her world. She needed him to get up so that this Sunday could be normal.

She was about to go out, when she turned back into the room. Reluctantly, but knowing that it was right and important on a Sunday and that God would be watching, she took a gap-toothed comb and pulled it through her tangled hair, her eyes watering at the tugging. Her hair came well past her shoulders now and the curls hung more heavily than when she was younger. Now they spiraled more than bounced and they sat more obediently under the tattered lace cap that she now attached to her head. She pulled the thin ribbon through the gathered edge and the ribbon broke, as she had been expecting it to do for the last few Sundays. Tying the broken ends together, she mended it as best she could.

Essie looked down at her feet, bare and toughened. Her dress was shrinking. No, she was growing, her legs lengthening and her long scrawny arms stretching through the sleeves like willow branches. Squinting into her broken piece of looking glass, she looked at herself as though at a stranger. Then grinned and stuck out her tongue. Life was too short to spend time staring into looking glasses.

Robbie did not get up. Essie went out, leaving her shoes behind—with the sun filtering down to the wider streets, it would not be cold enough to waste good leather. Robbie would be better soon, she told herself firmly. Her father had been drunk often enough for her to know what the morning after looked like.

The early sun was shining wetly on the pavements, the High Street smiling with people in their Sunday best. Girls and boys walking demurely behind their parents; servants, too, their faces scrubbed and ready for heaven. The ladies wore long gloves, the cuffs covered by short cloaks, their hair almost hidden by stiff bonnets. And their men strutted, stern in greatcoats.

Familiar faces called greetings to Essie and she waved back. A pieman, eyes open for any disapproving Calvinist who might wander by, slipped her a broken pie as she lingered near his barrow, her mouth watering at the beefy steam. She ate it hungrily. A dog began to follow her. She threw a piece of pastry as far as she could and watched a seagull snatch it before the dog could reach it. "Have tae be quicker than tha'," she told the dog. It still followed her, trusting, before it found a discarded bone and dragged it away somewhere.

She did not follow the Sunday-best crowd to the kirk. Essie's Sunday best was not good enough. The only difference in her clothes on Sunday was her lacy cap. Her dress was as clean as it could be, pummeled in cold weakly sudded water, and hung to dry on lines between the houses, or by the sooty fire when the rain poured down outside. But it was not nearly good enough for the kirk. No, barefoot Essie was going to listen to a preacher on the Grassmarket. She found herself a position, perched high on the top of the well so she could just see above the heads of the crowd. She could not hear properly everything that was being said, but she liked to watch the drama of the preacher's arms and catch snatches of the familiar words of justice, and see the crowds nod, their heads all turned toward the black-gowned beaky figure in the wooden preaching tent. She liked the way, when a drunkard shouted something, the crowd turned on him and some chased him till he fell in the gutter and lay, to become the object of the preacher's fury and the crowd's self-righteous laughter. It seemed right. It made sense.

All morning Robbie drifted groggily on the edges of sleep. It was many hours before he got up and when he did his lips were dry and gray, his stomach empty, his eyes still gritty. He stumbled blearily to get something to eat. There was no milk in the jug on the windowsill. The fire had gone out again and was now nothing but embers. Robbie kicked the table leg with his bare foot, his vision buzzing.

Footsteps on the stairs. The squeak of the opening door speared his head. It was Essie.

"You better now?" she asked. Robbie mumbled something. "Where were you last night?" she asked, her voice sharp.

"Mind your own business." He knew she deserved better. But a whisky head, mixed with his own guilt, made him angry.

"My ain business?" she spat, her words coarse as thistles. "How's it no' my ain business? We've barely money enough for food. Where'd you get money fo' drinking?"

Robbie looked at her, no words to answer her anger. He rummaged in the pocket of the trousers he was still wearing. He pulled out three coins and threw them on the floor.

Essie leapt on them, her fury blown away. She trod on one with her bare foot and as she bent to pick it up another was hidden under her skirts. Her fingers scrabbling, she picked them up and held all three in front of her, her mouth open wide, almost laughing. "Where d'you get these? It'd take us days tae earn these!"

"Give them back to me," he snapped. But Essie was still staring at them, twisting and turning them, wiping them on her dress, looking at each side. For one horrible moment, Robbie pictured himself in the cell again, with the crazy creature eating his coin. He grabbed them from Essie, accidentally scratching her hand.

She drew her arm back as though bitten. She looked at Robbie with disgust. He turned away.

"Take one," he said, "and go and buy us some food."

As she left the room, Robbie lay back on the bed again and closed his eyes against his headache.

Essie would have to grow up, he thought. It was a hard world out there and he was doing his best to survive. For both of them. If they did not help themselves, who else would? They had been deserted, by their mother, by their father, by God. They were up against the world with its injustice and its rich sneering uncaring Dr. Knoxes. And there were two choices: fight, or drown in the pig-swill slum. I am older than Essie, he told himself. I understand more of the world. She can go to her Sunday School if she likes, and listen to her preachers, and nod obediently at the words she hears, but I have found another way to fight, and to win.

Next day, ignoring Essie's shell-tight silence, he went about his work for Mr. Brown without her. And in the evening, when darkness cloaked the city's limbs, he turned his back on her again and went out. A growing excitement pulsed through him.

The door to the inn was closed but light spilled from the windows. Robbie paused, took a deep breath, and pushed open the door. He was again drawn into the thick warmth of the noisy room. Across the people, he immediately saw Hare, standing with his arm round a woman, his face buried in her ear.

Robbie tried to catch his eye. He felt a hand on his shoulder. Margaret. She leaned toward him, her slack smile revealing her browned teeth and holes where teeth had been. "Hello, pretty boy. What can I dae for ye?"

"Is . . . does Mr. Hare have any work for me? And Mr. Burke?"

"Mr. Hare? Mr. Burke?" she laughed, mocking his politeness. Her breath smelt of sweet ale and fish. He blushed, uncomfortable in her presence, not knowing what to say. She placed one finger on his lips and traced it slowly down his face, his throat, into the smooth cupped hollow in the center of his collarbone. Her soft, loose, sweaty body was too close to him. His breathing quickened. She seemed to sway toward him until her full lips were the closest part of her.

He turned away, stepped back. She laughed again, looking for a few long seconds into his eyes. "Saving yesel', then? For someone pretty?"

"No . . . I . . ."

"You dinnae have tae tell me. Why would I care? Wait here." And off she went, pushing between the crushed bodies toward where Hare and the girl were. On her way, many a man turned and touched her, whispered in her ear, stared at her breasts, tried to grab her. She dealt with them all with equal ease.

She reached Hare, spoke to him. He turned to Robbie across the sea of faces and shook his head.

Robbie left. Outside, with the door closed on him, he turned and looked through the thick silent window. The warmth, the laughing faces—he wished he could join them again. Wished he could be part of that drifting easy mindless world. Longed to bury his lips in that warm black ale, or to feel the bite of whisky as it flooded through his body and lifted him floating way way way above everything.

He did not go home straightaway. He could wait forever before returning to face Essie's accusing looks. What did Essie understand of anything? She was eight years old. A child.

Robbie walked slowly through the streets. No one looked at him. He could meld into the filth and darkness of the shadowed closes and no one would care what he did. Every now and then, a shaft of narrow moonlight found its way between the tall crazily stacked buildings, lighting up the ankle-deep human and animal waste that swelled overflowing from channels cut too shallow.

Dr. Knox did not live in a place like this. No, his genteel home was a delicate distance outside the skin of the stinking city, away from the houses piled on top of each other, sometimes sixteen stories high, lightless buildings squashed shoulder to shoulder, tall, thin and struggling to stay upright as they stretched dizzily toward a weak sun. Dr. Knox did not have to breathe the diseased stench from the bowels of the streets or dirty his shiny shoes in the blood and slime outside his own door.

And these doctors, these surgeons sauntering and smiling idly in the marbled air of Surgeons' Hall, what did they know of life in the real world? Nothing, thought Robbie, his jaw clenched. But he would make Dr. Knox be a part of his stinking world. He would sully him with the taint of stolen corpses. Robbie knew the corpses were stolen but what did that matter? He had not stolen them. He had done nothing wrong. It was all just part of the world he had been thrown into, through no choice of his own.

A clanging. Clattering, shouting. One of the new fire carts being pulled at speed by black horses came jangling round a corner, uniformed men running beside it. At the same moment Robbie smelt the smoke. He held his breath while he waited to see which way they would go. Away from his home they clattered, and he breathed again in relief. If you lived in the Old Town you had to fear fire even more than disease. Robbie had his own memory to fuel his fear.

Four years ago now, but he would never forget the deadly roar of the flames as they had swept through buildings and leapt high into the blood-orange sky. As the windows shattered and the wooden roofs puffed into ash, each building became a skeleton, revealing its flimsy structure, the emptiness of its frame. Like a body without its soul. Burning in hell.

They had been let out of school early and Robbie had stood and watched before going home. Transfixed.

Never would he forget the din, a crashing mixed-up chaos of every noise the world had heard of, so loud that for a while he could hear nothing at all, only see people shouting and beams and stone come tumbling silently to the ground. Then there was the confusion, the people running in all directions, the ladders, the human chains with leather buckets of water and dung, different people waving their arms with opposite instructions, even men fighting over who was in charge; the horses rearing, their mouths curled back in terror; women gawping, their silken bonnets protecting their hair from ash; the children staring wide-eyed and wide-mouthed or burying their heads in their mother's skirts. Most of all, he would never forget the sight of two people leaping from a seventh-floor window, holding hands, and their flaming rag-doll bodies tumbling like Catherine wheels to the ground.

Later, when the delicate tip of the steeple of the Tron Kirk came spinning silently through the flames, a despairing roar went up from the crowd and Robbie thought that truly the world was coming to an end. That nothing could ever be the same again.

Four hundred families lost their homes while the fires raged, and eleven people died. Not Robbie's home, not Robbie's family. The flames did not touch them. But they might as well have done. His father did not come home at the usual time, did not fling wide the door with a comforting smile. Robbie and Essie waited for him, wondering at first what present he might have brought them that day, then just wishing he would come himself, without a present.

Robbie could not bring himself to stoke their fire that evening. Did not dare. He raked the embers and let the glow die down to almost nothing.

They waited for two hours. Night fell. Robbie lit one oil lamp, watching it closely, never taking his eyes off the flame. He moved everything a safe distance from the lamp. He and Essie grew cold. They put on extra clothes. There was a thick mutton broth in the pot, left by Jeannie McKnight, the woman who came to look after Essie. They ate it cold. Just when they thought they could wait no longer, that they must find someone to help them, they heard footsteps on the stairs. Tired footsteps.

He came into the room slowly, his eyes white in a face streaked with soot, one sleeve of his jacket ripped from the shoulder. He went straight to a cupboard and took a bottle of whisky, pouring himself a large measure. His hands were black. For a moment he did not drink, just stared at the golden liquid as if drawing himself down into it. Then, with a deep breath, he quickly lifted it to his lips and drained it, in one desperate fiery mouthful. He squeezed his eyes shut and breathed out. A dribble of whisky trickled down his chin. He did not wipe it away and it left a clean pink channel in the dirt of his face.

Essie, from a dark corner of the room, whispered, "Father?" Robbie moved a little way toward her. The two children watched their father. Essie without comprehension, Robbie with fear. There was something wild in his father's eyes.

Essie spoke again, unafraid, a black curl escaped from her white ruffled cap. "Why you all dirty?" Their father did not look up, his head hanging down, the empty glass pressed against his forehead.

"What has happened, Father? We were worried," said Robbie.

"You were right to be worried," muttered their father. "What do you think has happened? Did you not see the fire? Did you not hear it?" His voice rose on a wind of emotion, his accent changing in despair as he spoke. "Have ye no' seen the buildings, collapsed, destroyed? All destroyed." He poured himself some more whisky and drank it furiously.

"Yes, I saw it." Robbie was angry. It was not his fault so why did his father make it feel like his fault? "I saw . . . I saw everything." As he spoke he tried to shut out the memories of what he had seen. "But we're safe. Our home is safe."

His father drained his glass and threw it against the wall, where it smashed into shocked silence. Then he roared, exploding, his voice thick with Scots now, "What the deil d'ye ken? It is the end, the end o' us, o' everything, it . . ." and he sank onto a chair, folded himself over and sat with his head in his hands, rocking. Robbie was almost certain that his father was crying.

It was not till the morning that they learnt the whole truth. Their father had left in the early hours and when Robbie went outside to look for him he met three angry-faced men looking for him too.

"Where's Mr. Anderson, lad?" demanded one, coming right up to Robbie.

"Out. He went out. Sir."

"Aye, weel, he needs tae come back quickly. He owes us money." The man jabbed a finger toward Robbie's face. Two more men arrived, flat caps pulled down tightly over their tired smudged faces. One had a charred sleeve and a raw black-edged weal on his hand, which he cradled.

"You looking fo' Anderson too?" one of them asked the first men.

It was Jeannie McKnight who explained. She came early that morning, her kindly face thick with weeping, her red sausage fingers enclosing Essie's startled face, as she looked despairingly at them both, shaking her head with incoherent cries of "The puir man! Wha's tae become o' us a'? 'Twas the deil's work, 'twas so!" Once she had calmed down, Robbie began to understand. His father had been the insurer for one of the seven-story buildings that had collapsed. Of his two business partners, one had died in the fire and the other had disappeared. They owed a small fortune. A fortune that they did not have.

Jeannie McKnight left. How could they pay her now? Many times before she went she took Essie in her saggy arms and wept more snuffling tears. "I would tak' ye, so I wuid. The baith o' ye. But ye ken I cannae. There's ma' ain family tae think o', an' ma' man no' weel." So she left, leaving them one last pot of rich beef broth before she went. It was the best beef broth they had ever tasted, thick with clumps of barley and stringy with onions, hiding huge lumps of melting beef and dark with a stock cooked for hours over her own hearth.

Now, more than four years after the fire, he could not forget. It was, after all, the reason why he and Essie now lived in a one-roomed hole with the reek of the flesh market beneath them.

As he walked slowly up the stairs once more, he could not ignore the crumbling decay and excrement all around him. He stepped aside to avoid the buzzing remains of a pig's snout halfway up the stairs. On the fourth floor, a door opened as he passed and one of the women fell out, screaming with laughter. She lay there, stranded on her back, one breast like an empty pig's udder hanging from her torn chemise. "Dinnae jist stand there, pretty boy!" she shrieked. "Gi'e us a hoist!" The stink of gin rose from her open mouth. As Robbie stood there, two more women lurched out of the room and grabbed the woman by her feet, shrieking with laughter as they dragged her back into the room. A frightened mouse scuttled out of her hair as she slid away, her white legs spilling from her footless stockings as her underskirt rucked up beneath her.

This was not how my life should have been, thought Robbie. It was hard to push the bitterness away. So much easier to be angry.

Next morning, before six o'clock as usual, Robbie made his way to the bakery through sheets of squalling rain. Passing the Flodden Wall, he took a tiny detour to look at the door. It was closed, thick, blank. A dog raised its scrawny leg

106

against the step and the piss steamed in the March morning darkness. Robbie hurried on to the bakery.

Mr. Brown looked at Robbie's gray face. "Ye a' richt, laddie?"

"Wha's tae be a' richt about?" Robbie grumbled.

"Aye, weel, it's a dreich day, so it is," said Mr. Brown with a nod, peering out of the dough-steamed windows. "But it's no' like ye tae be so dour, laddie. Ye'll need tae smile fo' the customers." The light from an oil lamp glistened on his high-domed forehead, its thick skin wrinkled back as though he had pushed it out of the way of his eyes.

Robbie glared at him and Mr. Brown turned away, too soft to speak out. Robbie loaded up all the different wheat breads, oat breads, barley cakes, oatcakes, bannocks, gingerbread with icing stained red with cochineal, pastries twisted and drizzled with treacle, bridies oozing gravy. He fixed the cover onto the barrow and set off, leaving the dough-hearted Mr. Brown to beat and pummel the yeasty mixture until the sweat shone rosy on his arms.

The rain seeped down Robbie's face and neck as he wheeled the barrow. He spent the day wet and cold, his mind numbed. His unsmiling face gained him no extra money. He bought a turnip and an old onion on the way home. Told Essie to make them into broth.

The broth was thin and gray. He added more salt from the wooden saut bucket crusting on the hearth. Wet wind blew soot back down the chimney into the room. The fire spluttered blue flames. Essie coughed, the phlegm black on her hand.

That night, Hare shook his head again and Robbie went home angry.

The week continued. Robbie and Essie barely talked, their silence cloud-heavy and cold. Essie watched him, anger gradually congealing into fear. Robbie was disappearing. Her world was changing. She did not understand the change that had come over her brother. Did not know words for what she felt. Just that it was frightening, like walking in a dark unknown street, faster and faster, far from home.

She did her best to keep their room clean, bring food back, wash clothes and hang them from the lines that cat's-cradled the narrow space high between the buildings. At first, she emptied the chamber pot in the proper way, walking downstairs whatever the weather, down the narrow wynd, and carefully tipping it into the communal midden. Soon she gave that up, tipping it out of the window like everyone else, her small voice shouting a warning with an increasing lack of care.

She stopped asking to go with Robbie on his rounds. His surly face and snappy voice were no pleasure to be with. Instead, she hung around the fires of the potato braziers or the chestnut sellers in the Grassmarket, with the other street children. She left her shoes at home. No point in wearing them out. Besides, the other children had none. And so she hardened, built a shell around her fear. But as she did, the sparkle in her magpie eyes dimmed, its energy burning up until it was little more than an ember.

Sometimes in the evening, when Robbie was not there, she took out her battered kaleidoscope from its hiding place under the bed and stared into its spiraling patterns until her head was filled with color. Then the ember in her eyes glowed more brightly, for a moment, before dying down again. Each time dimmer than before.

Each evening, Robbie went to Hare's inn. Each evening, he watched the crowded room of openmouthed faces, smelt the swill of ale and whisky and warmth, felt the easy touch of slack-lipped Margaret's hand on his arm and the conflicting feelings she aroused. Each evening, his heart sank as he saw Hare shake his head and turn back to his friends. And each evening, Robbie walked slowly back home, with nothing changed except his anger grown more bitter and more aimless.

He bought whisky and drank it under Essie's tight-lipped gaze. What did she know? A part of him, somewhere inside, remembered what they had both felt when their father drank whisky, and he knew Essie probably thought the same now. But that part of him, the part that had cared, was shriveling.

Then, at last, one night Burke met him at the door to the inn. His pale eyes were snake slits, his body rigid with tension, as he beckoned Robbie to hurry to the back of the building and meet him there. Excited, Robbie obeyed.

There was Hare, his lips wetter than ever, his arms jangling and restless. His right hand hovered near his coat pocket, sometimes resting on the knife hidden in it. His left tugged sometimes at his ear, then at his lip, then pummeled the edges of the twisted scar that ran past the corner of his smaller eye. He chewed frantically, the smell of dried fish salty on his breath.

There was the cart, a new herring barrel fastened with the rope. Robbie looked at it, fascinated. He thought of what was going to happen to the body inside it. He thought of a smiling Dr. Knox slicing smoothly into its cold flesh and peeling back the skin. His breathing quickened through his nose, and his lips tightened. A feeling of lightness threatened to lift him away and he tore his eyes from the barrel.

As before, Robbie ran in front of Hare and Burke, peering round corners, beckoning to them or halting them with gestures of his arms. Soon they were in front of the Flodden Wall. High up, the fluttering light from a window of Knox's anatomy school wavered as someone passed by. They waited till Robbie gave the all clear; then he hid as before and the two men pulled the cart to the door.

As before, Knox came out, the deal was done and two students rolled the barrel into the building, nervously looking around as they did.

Yellow gaslight fell on Knox's face as he turned. He looked like a corpse himself. Robbie's hatred was something hard and physical inside him. It seemed to grow, feeding off itself. He let it grow, needing it to create a meaning for what he was doing.

The three of them made their way back to Hare's inn, spirits high, drunk on success and on the money in their pockets. Robbie laughed with them, joking about the evil doctor and his disgusting habits. They all knew what he did, despite his fastidious clean fingers and the perfect elegance of his bejeweled velvet clothes, his delicately curled and pomaded side-whiskers and his musical voice. His pitted skin told a truer story, as though each scar was the outward sign of evil within.

What did he do with the parts when he had cut them into bite-sized portions? they wondered aloud. Did he serve them up to his guests? Hare acted the part of a butler, serving up a tray of delicacies to a lady, a part played with skill by Burke, who, with unusual jollity, stuck his chest out and wiggled his hips as he pretended daintily to eat an eyeball. They laughed. Robbie laughed too.

At the inn, they left the cart behind the house and went inside, arm in arm. Robbie felt himself folded into the warmth of the crowd and a smile spread through him as he flipped the lid of his tankard up and dipped his top lip deep into the ale. Noise steamed around him, wrapping itself about his ears, his head, his whole body, as he gave himself up to its holding arms.

The three of them joined Margaret, and Burke's wife,

Nelly, a cold dark-haired woman with sandpaper skin and bristles on her upper lip, whose eyes watched Robbie with something like mistrust. Robbie did not care. He did not care about anything, and soon Nelly's narrow eyes swirled into a haze, just like everything else. When someone spoke, the others laughed, about anything or nothing. It was the laughing that mattered. Laughing was belonging.

After the ale, the whisky, rich, amber and warming. Robbie fell easily into the cocooning arms of whisky and laughter. Arms that held him tightly, as if they would never let him fall. This was better than anything he could remember. Or there might have been something better, something warmer and more real and more important, but if there was he had forgotten it.

He rolled home a long time later, stumbling up the stairs in the pitch-blackness. The room was dark, too, the fire glowing dully. Essie was in bed. He climbed into their bed still clothed, his mouth leathery, his head spinning with something that had felt like happiness and now began to feel like something else, something heavier.

Essie turned aside and pulled the blanket over her head, shutting him out. She curled up in a ball. In the dozing moments before Robbie fell asleep, he could sense her wakefulness, could hear her fast breathing above the quiet hissing of the fire. He ignored it.

Next morning, Robbie was woken by Essie shaking him. It was daylight. He blinked, confused. "Wake up! Get up, Robbie!" she was shouting.

He groaned. A dangle of sticky saliva hung from his mouth. "Go 'way, Essie."

"But Robbie, you're late for work! What'll Mr. Brown say? I woke you afore and you went back to sleep while I was out getting water."

"Who cares?"

She shook him again. "Robbie, get up!"

Robbie sat up, clutching his head as he did so. He swallowed, wiped his mouth on the greasy sheet. "Can't you see I'm sick? Go and tell your Mr. Brown. He'll believe it from you." He lay back down again and pulled the blanket over his head.

"You're no' sick! You're drunk! You're nae better than our feckless father!" she shouted, her shoulders sharp under her dress as she tried to shake him.

There was no movement from the bed, no sign that he had heard. She ran from the room, crashing the door behind her. Robbie was alone.

Essie ran down the stairs, up the narrow wynd, her bare feet cold on the wet cobbles. The wind sliced through the watery sunlight and she wished she had brought her shawl or stopped to put her shoes on. Down the High Street she ran, made faster by anger and the need to act. She had to save Robbie's job. They needed his job. If he lost it, what would they do? How would they survive? Man did not live by bread alone, Essie knew from her Sunday School. But they would die without it, she knew for herself.

Into the Canongate now, past the prison on her left. She recoiled when she thought of Robbie locked in there. Then, nipping into a tiny street on the right, she wound her way round corners and came to the road where the baker's shop sat, its sweet malty smell making her mouth water. She slowed to a walk and approached the door, her chest heaving.

There was no barrow outside. She went in. Mr. Brown looked up, expecting a customer. His face fell when he saw Essie. He turned away, blushing, flustered. Wiped his fat fingers on the white apron wrapped around his barrel stomach. Reached for a piece of unbroken gingerbread, white-iced, snowcapped. And then a black bun, thick, warm, its rich fruitiness wrapped around by thin pastry. He handed them to her, not meeting her eyes.

"Ah'm sorry, wee Essie."

"Robbie's sick, Mr. Broon. He said tae tell ye. He'll be a' right the morrow, ye'll see." Like Robbie, she had the ability to change her accent on demand.

Mr. Brown, wiping his forehead, came round the counter. He crouched down with difficulty, hunched on his fat thighs. He avoided her face but he took her hands in his. He paused. "Nae, Essie. There's nae job for Rabbie. It's no' your faut. It's Rabbie. He's no' bin working weel, the past week or mair. The customers are no' happy."

"But Mr. Broon!" Essie's voice rose. "He's no' weel. Let me dae his work. I could dae it. He's no' that much stronger 'n me! Where's the barra? I'll show ye!"

Just then the door opened and they both turned. In the doorway stood a boy of about twelve, his nose dripping, crusted sores around his lips. A gallus grin, wide mouthed, hang-jawed. And Robbie's barrow in his hands.

"Done it, Mr. Broon! Quick, wis ah no'? An' I got ye a new customer. Hoose o' la-di-dah English lady an' all."

Mr. Brown stood up, dizzy from sitting on his thighs. Essie darted toward the door. Mr. Brown picked up the gingerbread and the bun. "Essie, no! Dinnae go. Mebbe I could . . . Tak' these at least. I'll no' hae ye starving." But

Essie was gone, leaving Mr. Brown standing agitated on his doorstep as he watched her run, bare feet flashing, toward the Old Town.

She did not go back home straightaway. The city was stirring, with people on their way to work in the icy early-morning gloom, and sprawling drunks rousing themselves and groaning. She wandered around the streets, cold to her bones. Drawn by the warmth, she stood near a potato brazier, forcing a smile to her face as she spoke to the pipe-smoking woman who handled the potatoes as though her hands were leather. The woman saw her red raw feet and stick-skinny arms and let her stir the fire with a metal rod. She gave her a large potato steaming from a slit in its skin.

Later, Essie found some of the street children she knew. Three boys were drinking gin from an earthenware flagon, tipping it into their mouths from a height. One of them threw a stone at an old lady passing. The boys laughed when it hit the old lady's ankle and she cried out in pain. Essie left them and went home.

Robbie said nothing at all when she told him about his job. He merely emptied the contents of his pockets in front of her and watched her face as she saw the coins fall. Her face showed nothing. She did not know what to think. Except that they would eat.

And so the days went by, unthinking. The weather lightened, the sun lifted itself higher, clouds whitened and dissolved, the distant sky between the towering houses deepened into a hopeful blue. Robbie noticed none of it. Every morning, he woke late, dragged himself headachy from his bed, spat thick phlegm out of the window, ate little, washed rarely. Sometimes Essie was there. Sometimes she was not.

His mind silted up. He was trapped in the airless narrow veins of the Old Town, under the weight of cold stone and sunless wet walls that ran green with bile. The city was sick and he had caught its sickness.

Sometimes, very occasionally, Robbie realized that this was not how his life should be. But none of it was his fault, he told himself. And if it was not his fault, what was he to do about it? So much easier just to chase the happiness that came from the whisky that he drank each night now in Hare's inn, because nowadays when Hare shook his head, Robbie just came into the warmth and drank late with the rest of them.

One night, in the inn, as his mind wandered during Hare's vitriolic ranting about his dismal life back home in Ireland, Robbie's eyes drifted round the room. He caught sight of a thin, hollow-eyed boy of indeterminate age gazing at him, his fair hair a tangled web on his shoulders, dirty strands dangling in his eyes, shadows on his skin. Though hard-faced, almost cruel-seeming, the boy did not look part of the crowd, his mind elsewhere, his smile unfelt. The boy looked lost.

Robbie took a mouthful of whisky. As he did, the boy took a drink himself, a large mouthful, gulped quickly and desperately.

As Robbie lowered his drink, so did the boy.

It was not a boy. It was a looking glass.

Robbie drank again and tottered home alone. Drunk though he was, as he climbed the stairs, he realized suddenly that what had felt like happiness before was nothing like it at all. He sat on the edge of the bed, his head in his hands.

Essie stirred where she lay. "Robbie?"

"Go to sleep," muttered Robbie. He lay down. He did not allow himself to wonder what she was thinking.

He closed his eyes and let his thoughts drift amongst the background noise of the night. Like an aged man, with grumbling stomach and stertorous breathing, the Old Town was never silent, and through the thin partitions and shared walls and damaged floors the shouts and crashes and wailing of babies mixed with the creakings of the rafters and the rattling of loose doors and windows. But Robbie was used to it. Soon he was asleep and the city breathed on.

The next time Hare and Burke had work for him was perhaps two weeks later. By now it was the end of April, not that Robbie noticed the increasing lightness of the evenings or the growing warmth in the sun by day. He simply stirred himself dully at the end of another day of blankness and left to make the familiar journey to Hare's, below the sullen shoulders of the castle.

At the inn that night, Robbie's heart leapt when Hare beckoned him round to the back again. Already, he felt the thrill of what they would do. Already he imagined the warmth of the extra whisky he would drink, euphoric once they were safely back at the inn, much richer.

Behind the building, there was no cart. No herring barrel slimy with fish scales. Hare and Burke seemed more nervous tonight, fizzing with needled tension. Their heads flicked from side to side, never resting. Even Hare, usually flushed with excitement, looked drawn and white as he chewed nervously.

Robbie began to speak, "Where . . . ?"

"Shut up and follow us, wid ye?" hissed Hare, his black eyes slits in the dark. "Not too close. We want to know if anyone's following."

Robbie knew better than to ask questions. There was something rat-violent in Hare's face tonight and Burke's eyes were little more than pale slits, his silence menacing. He followed at a distance as they walked, shoulders hunched in baggy coats, misshapen hats pulled down and collars high, through the streets, slippery shadows in the still night. He stopped at a corner, slid round it, waited, looked back. No one. No one other than those who should be there, going about their business.

Something stirred in a doorway. A bundle, shifting. A foot stuck from it. Just a drunk, relaxed as a rag doll. Nearby, a dead cat, stiff-legged. Robbie moved on.

Eastward they traveled, along the Grassmarket, then into Cowgate and under the new bridge, its graceful arches sweeping over the dank street toward the distant New Town. At first Robbie thought they were going to Surgeons' Square and Infirmary Street. Without a body for Dr. Knox? But no, they passed by and moved on swiftly.

Once, Robbie thought he had lost them. His heart pounded as he peered through the gloom. What would they do to him if—? But no—there they were. They took a narrow turning to the left. Up a steep slope, round a corner. Soon they were in the Canongate.

There, to his left, its windows like eyes frowning at him, was the Canongate Tollbooth, where he had spent a night he would never forget. He did not want to find himself inside again. He felt a prickling on his back.

Soon, the two figures stopped at a house, low and slumped, its roof sagging, its walls thick and uneven. They looked around, quickly opened the door and slipped in. The door closed behind them.

What now? Robbie waited for a minute, looking around,

hiding himself. No one had followed, he was sure. There were people passing, scurrying, heads down in the falling darkness. Two men shouted drunkenly at each other, face to face as they swayed closer. A woman picked through some rubbish a few yards away. But no one was watching Robbie. No one had noticed Hare and Burke go into the house. Quickly, he crossed the road. Knocked on the door. It opened immediately and he was pulled inside.

"Well? Anyone see us?"

"No, no one."

"You sure?" Hare's face loomed spittingly close. Robbie could see the fish rolling around his yellow-furred tongue. A blister seeped at the corner of his mouth.

"Yes, I'm sure. There was no one."

Hare let him go. "Margaret thought someone had followed us. Doesn't trust you, she doesn't. Sure, an' I might be agreeing with her. You wi' your lah-di-dah voice. And mind this," he said, pointing his finger within inches of Robbie's eyes, "ye're in deep as us, so you are. We hang, you hang." His face oozed sweat. His breath made Robbie gag.

Burke took over. He held Robbie's gaze with pearl-pale eyes, the near-white lashes almost invisible against his sallow skin. He looked like a slowworm, but with snake's venom. "Listen, we're nervous, is all. And wit' good reason, to be sure. We work from here now. Each night, you go to the inn as usual, but if Margaret or Nelly gives you the nod, you come here. You come here and you wait outside, hidden. You don't go in the house. You never go in the house if we're not here. You wait. And you don't get seen. Got it?"

"Let's git to work, an' fast," muttered Hare, wiping his hands on his trousers, over and over again. Burke led the way upstairs and Hare and Robbie followed. The wooden stairs,

118

little more than a ladder, creaked as they climbed. The walls were damp, and the smell of cod-liver candles and rotting vegetables sat in the air.

In a room upstairs a pile of straw lay in a corner, a gray pillow tossed on the floor beside it. Hare kicked aside the straw. There lay a man, a large man, slumped facedown, one knee forced beneath him, his arm twisted unnaturally out to the side.

"Help us wrap it," said Hare, picking up a large sack. "We've no barrel today."

Robbie's feet refused to move.

The two men were trying to turn the body over.

"Mary Modder of Jesus, wid you git over here and help us?" growled Hare, sweat breaking out again on his face.

Robbie moved, slowly as though in a trance. He grasped the man's jacket and tried to heave. The body was rigid. Suddenly, it moved, flopping over like a pig, and the trapped leg snapped free. The hand slid over Robbie's arm and, gasping, he picked up the wrist and flung it away from him. It hit the floor with a slap.

Hare had opened the sack and they began to pull it over the body's feet, bending the knees to force it in. Freed from its slumped position, the body flopped stiffly. The face stared up at Robbie, its eyes still open, the eyeballs webbed with broken veins, the tongue protruding through lips tinged with a blue-grayness. Or not really any color at all, just ghostly. As Robbie helped pull the sack up around the body, his fingers inadvertently touched the skin, the cheek, and he pulled his hand back quickly. The coldness shocked him, not the coldness of marble or anything hard—the coldness of earth. Not smooth or rough, not soft or hard, just dead.

They struggled to stuff the heavy body into the sack,

bending the stiff limbs roughly, and while they did so, Robbie noticed something. He stopped. The men looked at him.

"What's the matter? Too lah-di-dah for dirty work?" Hare looked darker than ever tonight.

"No," said Robbie, his thoughts whirring. "I . . . I was only thinking . . ."

"Aye, well, you'll leave thinking to others, so you will," snapped Hare.

"No, wait," said Burke, watching Robbie. "What were you thinking, I am wondering?"

"It's so clean," said Robbie.

"Clean? Stinks, so it does. Filthy, dirty tramp. Gutter food. Worth nothing alive." Hare kicked the body with contempt.

Burke put his hand on Hare's arm to silence him. He had not taken his eyes off Robbie.

"Why should it be dirty?" he said, his eyes straight slits, snake-still.

"I thought . . . because. From the grave."

"We are not grave robbers," said Burke slowly. "We wouldn't do that, so we wouldn't. Why would we be wanting to do that?"

Robbie was flustered. "I thought . . ."

"Aye, well, wid ye leave the thinking to others?" said Hare, stuffing the head into the sack and tying it with rope at the neck end. He was sweating, his eyes wild.

"Why do you tink the lovely Dr. Knox pays us so well?" continued Burke, still watching Robbie. "Would he pay us so well if the body was half eaten by worms, now? And he needs the bodies clean, fresh, so that he can do his bee-ootiful scientifical work. His careful and most expert cutting and slicing and pinning, sure an' he does."

"So, where . . . ?" asked Robbie.

"What you don't know about, you can't tell about," snarled Hare. "Mary Modder of Jesus, wid ye jist git a move on?"

"Sure, an' we get them from elsewhere. They had useless lives but they can be useful in death, so they can," Burke continued, still looking very carefully at Robbie.

"You mean . . ."

"Yes?" asked Burke, his hands slightly in front of and away from his body, ready. His eyes motionless.

"The gallows?"

"For sure," said Burke, his shoulders softening, his breath a gentle whistle. "The gallows. Criminals they are, layabouts, worth nothing alive. That's why they are so clean. They wash before they hang."

Not grave robbers then, realized Robbie. Not Resurrection Men. Somehow, Burke and Hare bought the bodies of hanged criminals and Knox was happy to buy the bodies to furnish his gruesome occupation. Because one body a year was not enough.

The man's neck had been covered, wrapped in a scarf. Robbie was glad. He had seen what happened at hangings. He would not have liked to see the neck.

With difficulty, the three of them carried the sack down the stairs. The limbs had started to loosen and Robbie could barely hold on to it. He was at the head end, and it lolled, leaden, flopping. Twice he heard a crack, felt the crunch of bones in the neck breaking under the head's own weight. He kept his lips clenched, his throat pressed tightly shut, his breath as thin as thread.

They heaved it onto the cart. A noise, a scuffling down an alley. They looked at each other, froze. Burke gestured with his head to Robbie. Robbie ran to a corner. In the distance, in the darkest shadows, perhaps he saw something, the flick of flying feet maybe, a scampering. Or nothing. Then silence once more. Or not silence. The city was never silent. Faraway shouting, the crashes of haphazard activity, singing, the rise and fall of human noise, footsteps ebbing and flowing. But nothing that concerned them.

"It's nothing," said Robbie. "No one."

"Mary Modder of God, will ye hurry?" muttered Hare, pulling his hat as far down over his black eyebrows as it would go. Both men grabbed the cart. Robbie ran ahead. Everything as before.

Once, when Robbie looked back to beckon them forward, for a moment he could not see them. They had stopped, had pulled the cart into the shadow of an archway. With frantic gestures of their arms, they beckoned him over.

"We're being followed!" whispered Hare.

"Over there—round that corner." Burke pointed to a turreted building, its steepled windows leaning out over the street, no lights burning inside. Cautiously, Robbie walked toward it, slid with his back against the wall and peered round. Nothing.

The wind whipped some paper fidgeting over the cobbles. A rat scurried from nowhere and disappeared behind an overturned box, rubbish spilling from it.

Distant noise and nearby nothing. Only Robbie's breathing. And now a wind that was rising fast, swishing in his ears and making it difficult to hear anything else. He turned his head this way and that, trying to catch any other sounds. Once he thought he heard something—footsteps?— but the possibility was whished away by the wind. Besides, why should there not be footsteps?

He turned back and retraced his steps to the men. They were worrying over nothing.

"There's still no one," he said.

On they went, quickly and silently, ears straining.

At the back of Knox's anatomy school, the usual routine—but this time with Knox looking inside the sack to inspect the body. This was now the third time Robbie had watched Dr. Knox hand over the money for his filthy trade. Each time, it seemed, his hatred grew. This time it rose like bile. Perhaps it was the extra tension of that night, perhaps it was that Robbie had seen, had felt, the body that Dr. Knox's knife would soon cut into. A cold wetness on his back and the smell of sweat from his own armpits.

As he watched Knox's mustard ugliness under the gaslight, it was all Robbie could do to stop himself running over and hitting him, hitting him, hitting him until he was as dead as the corpses he defiled.

Knox was arguing. Burke's face loomed toward Knox's, his neck rigid. The two students stood near the bundle, glancing at each other. They moved to pick it up. Hare leapt toward them, as if to kick their hands away. They rose angrily, bristled, moved forward boldly.

Burke pulled something from his pocket. A glint under the gaslight. It was a knife. He held it close to Knox's neck. Robbie's insides shriveled. He shrank further behind a tree, held his breath.

The students stopped, stepped slowly back, their palms facing forward. Hare had pulled his knife out now, Robbie saw, and it sliced the air between one student and the other. Hare moved toward them so that he was standing over the body. Voices rose but still Robbie could not hear what was said. Why were they not handing the body over? What was the arguing about?

The scene was frozen. Robbie wanted to run. Surely someone would pass by at any moment?

Dr. Knox moved his hand to his pocket. Burke grabbed his arm. Did Knox have a knife too? He would not hesitate to use it. Why should he hesitate? He cut into bodies every day, dead and alive.

Knox only smiled. Robbie could see his teeth. With his other hand, Knox slowly lifted Burke's hand from his arm, distastefully, said something that Robbie could not hear, and pulled something from his pocket. His purse. He gestured to Burke to move back. Hare still stood poised with his knife pointing toward the students. Burke moved slowly backward, watching closely, as Knox counted money from his purse. To Robbie, it seemed like more money than usual.

The scene melted: Hare moved back, and the students hefted the body and took it quickly inside. With his casual swan's-neck wave of the wrist, Knox slowly followed his students. Burke and Hare picked up the cart handles and ran together. Robbie followed. Through the streets they all ran, trundling the cart behind them. Only when they were far away from the Flodden Wall did they slow to a halt and turn to each other, roaring with laughter. They slapped Robbie on the back, their crazy laughter infecting him until all he could do was laugh as well, without knowing why.

Then they told him. Knox had paid even more money that night. They had told him they wanted more, that it was all too risky, that they had had to go to greater effort. They had reminded him that no one else could provide him with so many bodies, such fresh clean bodies, and that if he wanted

124

them to take risks he would have to pay extra for it. And he had—they had frightened him into it, boasted Hare.

Leaving the cart round the back of Burke's house, the three of them went on to Hare's inn, arm in arm, laughing, shouting raucously, weaving, dancing over the cobbles, jeering at passersby. People glanced at them and hurried on, heads down. It was as if they were drunk already— Robbie, too.

Soon, they were. Robbie fell into the warming chaos of the inn. He was one of the crowd, welcomed, and he laughed with the rest of them, throwing his head back as he drank. The storm of noise rose and faded, washing around him. He could not feel his legs, his arms, any external part of his body, only the fiery rush of the whisky as it flooded his insides. Quickly, his mind began to float and any fear, pain and sadness spun away into the distance.

Robbie stayed drinking long into the night. Why should he not? What was there outside those four walls? In here was shelter. In here he did not have to think about anything else. He drank more, though now it seemed harder to stay floating on that cloud-soft happiness.

Now the only way out was sleep because, asleep, floating or sinking made no difference. So, eventually, he slept, slumped on the floor of the inn, against the wall, his mouth hanging open, a string of saliva gently moving as he breathed. A man tripped and fell on top of him, a boot kicking his face as he rolled away. Robbie felt nothing. A dog urinated on him. He did not wake. Finally, as the other drinkers drifted home, a hand crept inside his clothes and stole the money from his pocket, all the reward for his night's work. He was unaware of any of it. He could have been dead.

In the early hours of the morning, he woke, rigid with cold. He was lying outside in the gutter, though he did not remember how he had got there. Pain shot up his arm as he freed it from under his head. His eyes throbbed and his stomach heaved. He vomited on the ground and the smell of it, whisky and vomit, made him vomit again. He retched and spat, while his head roared like waves.

Shivering and wet, he stumbled home. The night was still, the moonlight slicing between the buildings, and a slow floating smurr fell on his face.

By the time he reached his tenement and climbed the stairs, he was half sober. When he saw that Essie was not there, he became, suddenly, completely sober. Panic. The bed had not been slept in. His thoughts swirled and he struggled to make sense out of them. For a moment he stood, heart and mind racing but body paralyzed.

His own voice screamed inside his head. What had he done? He rushed down the stairs and back out onto the street. The rain now fell in cold sheets, a new wind whipping it around his face. Where could Essie be? In the grimy close, he called her name. The name echoed into the dripping emptiness. A dead cat stared up at him, its frozen eyes open.

On the High Street, he rushed from corner to corner, peering into every dark doorway. He saw a shadowed bundle curled under an archway. He ran, stooped over it. He pushed it and a white face peered out. A woman, quite young, stared at him with frightened eyes as though she was waiting for him to hit her. He covered her up again.

Out of the corner of his eye he saw it. A flash of brown as it flew toward his hand. Its eyes tiny circular beads. A rat, its yellow teeth bared. It leapt. He whipped his hand away. The rat missed his hand but landed on his chest with a shriek.

126

Swiping at it with his arm, he stumbled, fell backward, putting his other hand behind him to break his fall. As he landed, he felt, almost heard, something slice into his hand. He looked. Blood. Pumping, flooding from a deep cut at the base of his palm, toward his wrist. Mixing with the rain. Behind him on the ground a piece of broken pottery, one jagged peak covered in his blood. The rat slithered away, slipped over a wall and disappeared.

For a moment Robbie was too shocked to act. He stared at the blood bubbling out of his hand. It seemed to be flowing faster. He wriggled out of his jacket and wrapped it tightly round his whole hand, feeling a sickening almost-crunch as the flesh came together. Held his wrist across his chest. Stumbled to his feet. Took a deep breath to steady himself. Pushed the pain away. And ran back out onto the main street.

A few people were beginning to stir, workers who had to rise early, shopkeepers, traders, hunched under the rain. He saw a man he recognized.

"Have you seen my sister?" he asked.

"Who're you?" asked the man.

"Robbie. Anderson. Fleshmarket Close. Top floor." The man sniffed but said nothing. "My sister? Essie? Small, thin, 'bout eight years old, curly black hair?"

"Ah've no' seen her. An' ah dinnae ken ye," muttered the man, and hurried away.

Robbie ran to the next close. The world was a tunnel, black, jumbled, the pinpoint of light at the end disappearing. He searched everywhere, running, his thoughts shrieking. Essie! Where are you? Essie, I'm sorry! I'm so sorry! He did not know whether he spoke aloud or if the cries were in his head.

Driven by a fear that was a million times worse than anything Dr. Knox could do, he ran into every close, almost blind with panic. He bumped into people, grabbed strangers and asked if they had seen his sister. Everyone turned away, hurried on, disgusted by the disheveled bloodstained boy who reeked of whisky and vomit, whose hair covered his face, whose clothes were sodden and whose eyes burned like a madman's.

Eventually, there was nowhere else to look. He slowed to a halt and slumped in despair. His mind in an exhausted blur, he put one foot in front of the other and made his way home. There was nowhere else to go. Perhaps she would be there. She must come back. He thought his heart would crack.

His hand throbbed inside the jacket. He barely noticed.

As he approached the building, he stopped. Dimly, confused, he realized that two people were walking in front of him, starting to go up the stairs before him. He stopped, focused. One was Essie.

7

Joseph

"Essie!" he shouted, and began to run. Essie turned. The young man with her turned. Robbie stopped. He looked from Essie to the man. Essie stood in silence, as if torn between emotions. She walked hesitantly toward Robbie. He wanted to sweep her in his arms but there was too much now between them. He knew exactly what he had done. A river had been crossed.

"Essie," he said. "I have been looking for you. I see that this gentleman has brought you home safely." The formality of his words disguised the earthquake inside.

"I suppose you are Robbie?" asked the man. Young, perhaps eighteen, tall, straight-backed, his dark polished hair tied behind him, clean-shaven. A student, from his clothes. He stared straight at Robbie. As if assessing him.

"Yes—and you are?" asked Robbie, a wary politeness while he felt his way.

"My name is Joseph. You should take better care of your sister."

"Essie is tough," said Robbie.

The young man laughed. "Tough? Tough enough, for certain, to pick a poor student's pocket!"

"Essie!" exclaimed Robbie. She stared back at him, her chin jutting.

"It is not Essie's fault. What is a child to do for food when her mother is dead, her father has disappeared and now her brother, who used to care for her, has run off without a thought? Yes, I know all that. It was two days ago she tried to steal from me. This morning I found her picking food from the rubbish in the gutter."

Robbie felt exhaustion overwhelm him. His hand had begun to hurt properly now, pulsing with pain. His head swam and he wanted to sit down. He wanted to put everything back together again. But how was he to start?

"I'm sorry," he said to Essie, weakly, broken into tiny pieces. "I'm sorry, Essie. Now, shall we go inside?" He stood at the door and turned to Joseph. "Thank you—for bringing Essie back. And for not . . ."

"What has happened to your hand? You are covered in blood."

"It's nothing. Just a cut."

"Let me look." Joseph walked toward him. His eyes were narrow and gouged deep above high-set cheeks. His face was chiseled, carved from granite, perfect, symmetrical. He was different from anyone Robbie had met. Strangely confident. Simple clothes, yet an aristocratic line to his jaw. His coat, though long and well cut, was not new-looking. His waistcoat was a sober gray, his cravat unfussy, without a jewelled pin. And yet his voice suggested a wealthy education, its vowels long, its accent as English as was fashionable.

Robbie just wanted him to go. He did not want to owe this man more. "It's nothing, I told you."

"There's blood a' over, Robbie," said Essie, looking closely at his jacket.

"I am a medical student," said Joseph. "Let me look. You can die from a cut if it is deep enough."

Robbie stood still. "No, I can't . . ."

"If you are fretting about payment, think nothing of it. I am a student, I told you—I would welcome the practice. Most patients insist on an experienced doctor." He took Robbie's arm and held it up as he began to unwrap the jacket, with long delicate fingers. As he peeled away the last bit, his eyes narrowed. He wrapped it up again quickly. "That requires to be sewn. I shall fetch what I need. Which floor are you on?" Essie told him, and he nodded, as though he had guessed.

They watched him go, picking his way around the rubbish at the bottom of their steps.

Robbie and Essie went up the stairs in silence. Robbie had to hold the wall as he went, fighting back nausea. His head pounded.

Their room was a mess, crusted with neglect. Rubbish on the floor, an unwiped wooden brose bowl on the table, the bed a limp gray tangle, one candle slouched in a greasy tin. The ashes damp and cold in the grate. The window clouded, sunless. The smell of old food, something dead, whisky and vomit. What have we come to? wondered Robbie. What have I come to?

He sat down, cradling his hand against his chest, shoulders slumped. Essie stood warily, wordlessly, near the door, her face streaked with exhaustion. Robbie tried to gather together some words, though none could describe what he felt.

"I'm sorry, Essie. You will never know how sorry I am. I

don't know how this has happened. I'll change, Ess. It will all be all right, you'll see."

"So, you'll no' drink anymore? You'll no' come home drunk again?" Mistrust in her face, her clouded face, the eyes dull now as the ashes in the grate.

"No, I promise," said Robbie, as he had heard his father say before. Meaning it, perhaps as much as his father, perhaps more, perhaps enough.

"And you'll no' do that work anymore?"

"It's good money, Essie. We need the money, don't we?"

"What's on the cart?"

Robbie held his breath. "What do you mean?"

"What's on the cart?" Essie said more loudly, as though it had been kept screwed up inside. "Who're they two men?"

For a few seconds, Robbie could not speak. Then, slowly, quietly, "You followed me."

"Aye," came the small strong voice.

"Do not ever follow me again," said Robbie. He stood up and towered above her. His voice rose. "Do not ever follow me again! Do you hear? Stay away from those men. Stay in the house at night and don't *ever* follow me again!" Fear made him angry.

But Essie did not flinch. She stood as tall as she could and shouted back, "Why? What's so secret that it has tae be done in the middle o' the night and makes you so feared?"

He breathed deeply. He walked over to the bed and sat down. It felt as though the strength was washing out of him, leaving him hollow. "I'm so tired, I can't think."

"But what were you doing, Robbie? What were you doing with the men? An' who's the man what came out o' the wall? You must o' been doing something bad."

"Trust me, Essie. I did nothing wrong. Anyway, it

doesn't matter because I'm not going to do it again. I'm not going anywhere near those men again." As he said it, he felt his mind lifting. A haze of light in the distance.

Essie was looking at him, wanting desperately to trust him. Robbie went over to her and met her eyes and suddenly pulled her to his chest with his good arm and held her tight. Her cheek lay against his blood.

She struggled. "You reek!" she said.

Robbie knew that he did. "Well, we'll need water then, won't we? And a clean shirt. And after that, food. Well, food for you. I'm not hungry. I need your help, Ess."

"I'll get water," said Essie, glad to be able to act. She fetched the buckets and ran out of the door to go downstairs, her tiredness falling away. Robbie was back and he said everything would be all right. She wanted to believe him.

Robbie sat down again. Exhausted, weak. His head drumming. Weighed down by something that once again seemed too heavy to lift. And then another feeling, a feeling that snuffed out the shimmer of hope he had seen in the far distance. He needed a drink. He went over to where his whisky was kept. Took a quarter-full bottle, and pulled out the cork with his teeth. With a shaking hand, he poured a measure into a dirty cup. His body began to calm, to slow, to warm, as he thought of the flying feeling that would come soon after the fire hit his stomach. But as he lifted it to his mouth, he saw in the corner of his eye a movement. He had caught sight of himself in their piece of looking glass. There was that filthy, lost, sad boy, the one with serpent hair and dead eyes and white teeth in a dark face, like bones dug from the ground by a dog.

He looked at the cup in his hand, stared into the golden drink. He saw in it his father, a broken, useless man. That was what he would become if he did not grasp hold of himself.

He forced his arm to pour the contents of the cup into the chamber pot and tipped the rest of the bottle after it. And as he poured the whole pot out of the window with a loud cry of warning, the weight lifted further and there was suddenly just a little more light.

Footsteps on the stairs. Essie and Joseph. Joseph carried a brown leather bag, which he set down on the table, sweeping aside the dust and rats' droppings and the oatmeal-encrusted bowl.

"Get the fire going and some water heated, Essie, please, if you will."

"What's that for?"

"For your brother to wash himself. He reeks like your streets."

Essie set to work setting the fire in the hearth, her shoulders softening as she did her familiar work. She worked quickly, her fingers skillfully building a tiny mountain of straw and dried heather and striking the flint until the sparks caught the tinder.

Joseph opened his bag and took out a leather pouch. He began to unwrap it. Robbie spoke. "You said 'your streets.' Are you not from Edinburgh?"

Essie spoke up, her face shining. "Joseph comes from the country, Robbie. He's from a place called the Kingdom o' Fife. Everyone in the Kingdom o' Fife has houses, with more 'n one room each. An' they grow food in a garden, an' Joseph's house has water inside, that comes from the wall whenever you want it."

"I think you have your answer, Robbie," said Joseph, smiling.

"Essie seems to know you well," said Robbie, wondering how she could have found out such information.

"I confess that I have given Essie more than one meal in the last two days. You may wonder why I did not call a constable when I found her hand in my coat pocket. Usually, I would have done so. But Essie is . . . I can only say that I could no more have done so with Essie than I could have handed my own sister over to the magistrates. I had a sister once. She would have been Essie's age now."

They watched Essie hanging the pot above the crackling fire.

"Typhus," said Joseph, his face unmoving, staring into the flames. "She fell ill on a visit to an aunt in your town. The aunt died too. And two of her own children. It was a long time ago." Robbie said nothing. What could he say? It was a common story.

Joseph moved, shook his head, relaxed his face. "Sit down, Robbie," he said. "Move your arm as slowly as you can. Close your eyes and keep still." His voice was calm, reassuring. Robbie sat on the bed, his free will gone. He was happy to be doing what he was told. It was like being stroked inside his head, mind-melting, fuzzy-edged. He could feel his arm being unwrapped gently, sense the trickle of blood along his wrist, feel it wet on his leg. As his back sagged and his shoulders relaxed further, he could hear sounds of Joseph searching for what he needed. Heard the table being pulled over toward him, felt his arm being placed on the table. Then some tugging, pulling, on his wrist. No pain. A tiny stinging sensation that seemed to come from somewhere else. Somewhere drifty. Somewhere warm.

Sounds of another world clattered in the distant streets

below, in other rooms, on other stairs, through other windows.

"Essie, if the water is warm yet, mix a little with this, please." A minute later the sensation of something sticky being pasted over his hand. Still he kept his eyes closed. He felt his hand being bandaged tightly.

"I have finished. You should eat now. And wash."

Robbie opened his eyes. His hand was cleanly bandaged. He did not know when he had last seen a cloth so white. Soon the water was hot enough and Essie brought it, her tongue poking out as she concentrated on not spilling it, and he washed as best he could, stripping his shirt off in front of the fire, carefully easing it over his bandaged hand. Essie passed him everything he needed, knowing without being asked.

Joseph spoke as he put away his equipment in the leather pouch. "You live alone?"

"Yes." Little point in mentioning a father who was more useful gone. "But we manage."

"Is this what you call managing?"

"No, this is . . . This is not how it is."

"But what about Essie? She needs—"

"Yes, I know what Essie needs," snapped Robbie, shame making him angry. "I am sorry. But you know nothing about us." He felt awkward in front of this confident young man who was only a few years older and yet seemed to know so much more.

"I know what I can see. I can see you were drunk last night. I know you leave your sister alone at night. I can see that you live on the rotting top floor of a crumbling tenement, where typhus killed twelve people last winter, where humans and rats and pigs and dogs live as though none was a jot better than another. Where I come from, you would have a minister or some good lady of the parish calling at your door to save your souls. If not your bodies. God will provide and God will punish, they would tell you."

Robbie curled inside. He tried to keep his voice level but mention of God goaded him. "God? Where is God? What does God care about the likes of us?"

"Robbie!" shouted Essie, shocked. People burnt in hell for less than that.

Joseph picked up his bag. He turned to Robbie and looked at him closely. "Difficult questions, Robbie, but exactly the ones I would ask if I were in your position. Just where is God in all this?"

Essie's cheeks were white, her eyes wide. Robbie's thoughts raced, faster than he could grasp. Here was someone who was daring to voice his questions aloud.

Joseph was speaking again. "A baby died in the next building last week. Her older brother came to me, crying, to ask if I could do anything. A rat was eating the baby's face while it was still alive, the mother too weak to notice. The baby's breath reeked of gin and it was too drunk to care what was happening to it. There was nothing I could do. Where was God then?"

Joseph walked to the door. He turned to them. A smile, so straight, so slight. "Are you waiting to see me struck by a thunderbolt?"

Essie's hands were clenched. "God is watching. He is watching all o' us."

"You may be right, Essie." His voice was level but Robbie could tell he did not believe what he was saying.

"We don' understand everything," insisted Essie. "God decides, that's all." Robbie was silent.

"Take care of that hand, Robbie," said Joseph. "And of your sister."

Before Robbie had a chance to thank him, Joseph had left. Essie made herself busy at the fire, a frown clouding her forehead, her jaw tight. She said nothing. Robbie looked at the closed door and listened to the footsteps as they went down the stairs. He wanted to call Joseph back. He wanted to ask the questions that for so long he had kept inside.

Essie found Robbie his other shirt. The cloth was crumpled and thin, but clean, the worn threads soft and familiar. She held it out to him and he put it on.

He went to the window and opened it. The sunlight slanted onto the building, just a few inches from their window. It never quite shimmered into their own home, throwing its warmth into the spidered corners. A pair of curlews swung fast above his head, their mewling cries soaring, flying free. Down below, the street was in shadow; all the streets he could see were in shadow, darker and darker as they moved further away into dismal alleys and stinking gutters that the sun never reached. But up here you could see the sunlight, and freshness, and warmth, and smell a promised summer.

Essie handed him a bowl. Brose again. He was not hungry. He took a few small spoonsful of the watery oatmeal, under Essie's dull eyes. Soon, he stood up. Still they had not spoken about what they had heard. For both of them, it was too enormous.

"I have to go out, Essie."

"No!"

He turned away from the pain in her face. "I have to go and say thank you to Joseph." It was true—he had not thanked Joseph.

"I don' like him." She scowled.

"You liked him fine before, Essie. When he helped you. Besides, you're not coming to see him."

"Be quick, Robbie, an' don' . . . don' listen tae his bad words."

"A fine one to talk about bad words, you are! You've been stealing, Essie. What do they teach in Sunday School? Thou shalt steal?"

"It's different. Where am I tae get food for the both o' us when you're drunk?"

"Just tell me where he lives, Essie. I'll be back before you've read a chapter of your Bible."

Reluctantly, she told him and he left her standing there, silent and confused.

Only two streets away, another narrow close. The second floor. The stairs clean. Robbie knocked on the door. Joseph looked at him, without seeming surprised. "Do come in, Robbie." His confident politeness was unsettling. His eyes always steady, direct.

The room was clean, with thick green curtains pulled back from a wide window. Sunlight cutting through at a sharp angle. A dark polished table, four chairs, no bed to be seen. A strong fire crackling, a copper kettle hanging above the flames from a shiny clean rantle-tree.

"I came to say thank you. For this," and he held up his hand.

"I told you," said Joseph. "I was content to have some practice. My needlework needs improvement."

"And for not taking Essie to the magistrates. She . . ." But

Robbie's voice trailed off. His eye had been caught by something.

A violin. Lying on a table. Joseph saw where he was looking. Robbie spoke, the breath hovering in his throat. "Do you . . . do you play the violin?" Not taking his eyes from it. Wanting it. The memory so strong that it hurt.

"No, it is not mine. It belongs to someone else. I took it to be repaired nearby and the owner has yet to collect it." Joseph watched Robbie, seeing his fascination. "You can touch it if you like, but be careful. It is valuable."

Robbie touched its shiny yellowed warmth. He picked it up in his left hand, tucked it under his chin in one swift movement. He closed his eyes to the feel of it, the rosin smell, a memory of his mother. He opened his eyes again. If only his right hand was not stiff with bandages.

"You have played a violin, have you?" said Joseph, surprised.

"A long time ago."

"If it were not for your hand, you could have played that one."

"Whose is it?" asked Robbie. Wishing he could be that person. Could touch his world.

"Dr. Robert Knox. He is an . . ."

The power of that name! The breath spun from Robbie's body until it was as thin as spiderweb.

If he could, he would have gathered up that name and hidden it in his hands, squashing and squashing and squashing until it was tiny as a speck of dust, until it crumbled into nothing and was no more. He would have turned back time, not to hear Joseph say that name.

The violin slipped slowly from Robbie's hand. Joseph

leapt to catch it before it fell. He put it carefully on the table. Now Robbie could see that it was familiar. His mind was numb.

Joseph spoke. "You know the name?"

Robbie nodded.

"How do you know Dr. Knox?" His voice light, simply interested.

Robbie hesitated. "He killed my mother."

There was a silence. Then Joseph's voice cut coolly through it, his dark eyes hooded. "Dr. Knox is a skilled surgeon. If your mother died, it was despite Dr. Knox's best efforts, I am sure."

"He killed her! He cut into her alive and she screamed and screamed and I heard her. I was outside the room. I was eight years old. Dr. Knox killed my mother!" His voice rose, its notes lifting to a childlike pitch.

"Dr. Knox is the best surgeon in Edinburgh. Perhaps even Scotland. Surgery is dangerous. More than half of all patients die. We do not know why. I am sorry about your mother, but you cannot rightly blame Dr. Knox." Joseph's back was to the window. He was silhouetted. The spring sunlight sliced through the clean glass.

"I can blame Dr. Knox. I do." Robbie's voice grew louder on his anger. "He is the cause of everything that has happened to me. And to Essie. We had good lives before. We didn't live in a—what did you call it?—a rotting tenement. We were moving, to the New Town. To a house like the one your Dr. Robert Knox lives in. Everything would have been different if he had not—"

"He performed an operation on my mother too."

"And he saved her life, did he?" Robbie snapped.

141

"No, she died. That is why I chose to become a doctor. To try to save lives. Heal people. Like other doctors."

Silence. A red mist swirling. The words Robbie needed were stuck somewhere. His thoughts tumbled between guilt and anger.

"But he doesn't care about people!" Robbie struggled to find a reason to heap the blame on Dr. Knox. He needed that. "He cuts into bodies. Dead or alive—he doesn't much care. He only cares about the noise they make. I heard him say so. He digs his fingers in dead men's bodies. He cuts them open and pins the skin back and leaves them lying for men to peer into. I've seen it!"

"It is called anatomy, Robbie. You know nothing about it." Joseph's cheeks were tight, clenched, angry. There was a sharpness to his voice now. "You people know nothing about what we do. How else can doctors learn how to cure people if they cannot know what is inside a body? I have been to his demonstrations. I have even helped him. He teaches students. And he is the best teacher we have. He is inspiring." His voice ringing out, strident, inflamed.

Robbie could not speak. He needed his hatred of Dr. Knox, needed the knife-sharp anger to keep away the pain, but Joseph was blunting it. If he could not hate Knox, what would that leave him with?

Into the silence, Joseph continued, his voice softer now, his anger quickly gone. His calm control back. "So, what do you intend to do with your life, Robbie? You are clever. I saw the books—Latin and Greek. They are not your father's, are they? Essie would not tell me how you earn your money, only that you lost your job in a bakery. So, what are you going to do? Are you going to settle into the filth, and scrabble for your food under the feet of other people?"

142

"What choice do I have? What is there for someone like me?"

"There is always a choice." Joseph walked over to the fireplace. He was busy with something, lifting the kettle, scooping something from a tin.

Into the empty moment, the small space between them in this room, Robbie found himself speaking. It did not sound like him. It was as if the words were being pulled smoothly from him on a thread. Or someone else was saying the words while his mouth moved.

"There was something else."

"Yes?" The quiet sound of water pouring.

A deep breath. "What you said. About God." Silence. Robbie continued, fast now, words tumbling. "I can't talk to Essie. She goes to Sunday School and she can read the Bible. She seems to understand. But I don't. It was what you said about the baby. The one who died, eaten by a rat. What sort of God would let that happen? What sort of a God would take my mother?" The sentence hung in the air, dangling like a noose. At last, he had said it. The question he had kept buried for six years. What would happen to him now?

Joseph came over to Robbie, holding two steaming cups on saucers. The same blue-and-white pattern Robbie had seen at Knox's house. "Sit down. Drink this tea."

The thin porcelain edge of the cup slipped between Robbie's lips. His tongue touched the smoothness of it. The tea was strong and bitter, but sweet too.

Joseph trapped him with those steady eyes, smiled again that perfect smile. "How do you know it was God?"

"How could it not have been God? God decides, makes everything."

"No, I am asking you, how *could* it have been God?"

"I don't know. I don't understand the question. That's why I've come here. Because you seem to know."

"No, I do not know. I do not know what God is, or if He is at all. I will tell you what I *do* know. I know that I have not been struck by a thunderbolt, though plenty of people would like to see it happen when they hear what I say. I know that it makes no sense to me that God controls everything and yet rats eat a baby. How can a world so full of horror and mistakes be created by God?"

"But if God didn't make the world, who did? How could something so complicated create itself? Someone must have designed it."

Joseph's eyes shone. "Hah! You are using a well-known argument. You think because something is complicated it must have been designed. Why?"

"Because it makes sense!"

"The fact that it makes sense does not make it true. Let me tell you a story. It is not my story. A great philosopher, Mr. Hume—a native of Edinburgh, I may add—relates it. There was once an Eastern prince, he said. One day, a traveler from Europe told this prince that in his country the water in canals becomes solid when it is very cold. So solid that an elephant could walk on it. The prince was angry and said to the traveler, 'I used to believe everything you told me. Now I know that you are just a liar.' Do you see the point?"

"No."

"The only way the prince could make sense of what the traveler told him was to assume that he was a liar. The truth—that water can freeze solid—made no sense to him. So he chose to believe that it was not true."

Robbie's head was spinning. "But perhaps God is the

truth, and the truth just doesn't make sense to you? You just can't imagine God, like the prince not being able to imagine the ice. You might be wrong, like the prince."

Joseph grinned. He hit the table with his hand. "Clever lad! Perhaps you are right. However, I cannot go through my life struggling to believe something that seems to me to make no sense, and have no value. I avoid religion. I do not trust it. And now, Robbie, you should go back to Essie. She will be wondering where you are. Look after her—there is something special about her. Something in her eyes. Any other girl would have been in front of the magistrates long before now."

Robbie stood up. "I don't want her to know I have talked to you about this. She needs to believe."

"That is true for most people, Robbie. As Mr. Hume said, man created God for his own comfort. If Essie is comforted, then God has had some purpose." He followed Robbie to the door. "What are you going to do?"

Robbie looked around the room, at the books, the solid furniture, the sunlight. He looked at Joseph, the medical student who was making something of his life. He looked again at the violin, remembering his mother. "I have not decided. But I know where I shall start." And he did. He knew what he was going to do that evening.

"Goodbye, Robbie. Come again. Take care of your hand. Do not try to use it. Keep the bandage on—the air is full of evil. If the wound begins to smell, come back to me. Remember—I need the practice." Joseph smiled. Robbie had forgotten about his hand. It did not hurt at all.

*   *   *

Walking up the stairs to his room, Robbie was hit by exhaustion. Everything had washed out of him and he felt as weak as skin.

Essie looked up as he came back in. She was stirring something in a pot.

"I've made you some broth, Robbie. An' I've no' burnt it. An' there's bread, too." For Essie, survival was measured in food. But there was more to living than that. Man does not live by bread alone, as he remembered from his Bible. He smiled to himself with the beginning of understanding.

He did not want to eat, though he found that when he did eat he was hungry. "It's good, Essie."

"It's the best I've ever made," she said, spooning it fast into her own mouth and wiping the back of her hand across her lips. In the familiar act of eating, something of her strength and hope returned. Something in her began to shine again.

Afterward, Robbie climbed into bed and let his body sink onto the familiar straw-rustling mattress. He closed his eyes. At first he could not sleep—his thoughts were webbed like veins. It was hard to shake off completely the hopelessness he had felt only a few hours before. But now it was possible to believe that all would be well. That he could begin to climb back up to the air, to the rooftops, away from the slime and the sewers.

He knew what he was going to do.

He would go to Hare and Burke and tell them that he could not be involved anymore. He would say that someone was suspicious of him, had spotted him—which was true enough. They would surely not want him to work with them if he had been spotted?

Everything could go back to the way it was before. He would find new work, return to his studies, prepare for university, move toward a better future. For him and for Essie. As Joseph said, there is always a choice.

And so, believing, Robbie slept a dreamless, peaceful sleep.

8

A Glimmer of Light

Much later that day, Robbie woke. At first muddled. Then everything swirling into place. He rubbed the sleep from his face, and got up. The room was transformed. Books in piles, their few kitchen items on a shelf. Rubbish gone. The table almost clean, the window open and air washing through, catching the flames in the fireplace and making them lean as they fluttered.

Essie saw him. "I've some more o' that broth," she said. The sparkle kindled briefly in her eyes again. And then was gone, replaced with a memory of caution.

"Thank you, Essie. And well done—our room looks fit for a lord now."

As he ate, she sat on a stool nearby and slowly, with unpracticed fingers, braided her black hair into a thick uneven plait. She had not cut her hair for months and the curls had become waves, hanging down her back. Now, trapped by the braid, the waves were still. Her face seemed longer, her jaw stronger. When she smiled, her mouth moved more slowly than he remembered, as though she had to think through the act of smiling. "What're ye going to do?"

"I'm going to tell those men I'm not working for them anymore."

Relief leaping in Essie's face. Then fear again. "What happens if . . . ?"

"Nothing can happen. I'll just tell them that my family are suspicious. They won't want anything to do with me then. There's nothing to worry about—you'll see. Stay here until I come back."

Robbie picked up his jacket and, taking one last look round his home, he left the room. He turned again and smiled at Essie before he disappeared down the stairs. His last sight was her worried face, the braided hair flat over her ears. Somehow, he had to make it right for her. He could not watch her lose her trust, her spirit.

Once out of the building, he stopped. His hand throbbed. He leaned against the wall and breathed some strength into his body. It was late afternoon, and the gray April sun hung low in the sky, thinly veiled by cloud, but just visible between the zigzag leaning walls of two buildings. Time to go. Time to tell Burke and Hare that he could not, would not, help them anymore.

He moved off quickly, in the direction of Hare's inn. He did not know which house he would find them in but Hare's was nearer. The streets were noisy, filled with the jangled clamor of people's lives. From each direction, men and women of every class, clattering carriages, horses, dogs, all melded together. Children ran barefoot, or stood mucus-faced on corners, staring emptily. Soldiers sauntered, muskets loose against their chests, red coats splashed like blood across the rat-gray streets. A drunken woman lay sprawled against a wall, glassy-eyed, her baby weakly wailing as it tugged at her limp breast. Muscled Highland porters, strong as ponies, shouted as they pulled the sedan chairs, weaving through the crowds, the wooden staves resting across their shoulders. Traders cried their strange advertisements, their voices like trumpets over the sea of people. "Strongest whisky here! Drunk for three bawbees! Cold deed for five!"

Above all this rose the castle, sprouting from its rock like a giant's head above a diseased body. The veins of the city's streets pulsed filth, its buildings sweating waste, so that the whole creature reeked of illness.

Hare's inn, the windows cold and empty. Robbie knocked on the door. After a few moments, a woman came out, bleary-eyed, her clothes hanging loose, one shoulder bare. Not Nelly or Margaret, but whoever it was recognized him. "Ye want Hare? Try William Burke's hoose." And she closed the door.

A fast walk uphill, and then downhill. Soon, he stood outside Burke's house. Its windows quiet, its insides dark. He knocked on the door. The silence grew.

He knocked again. Waited. Nothing.

He looked upward. Something moving in a window?

There was someone in the house. He felt it. He knocked again, as loudly as he could. The door swung open, pushed by the force of his knocking. No one stood behind it. Robbie stepped inside. "Mr. Burke?" he called, but quietly. And listened. Nothing.

He was about to leave when he heard something. Unmistakable. A thud, followed by a scuffling sound upstairs. What was happening? Without thinking, Robbie ran to the wooden stairs and climbed them quickly, in one breath.

Flung open the door.

A frozen scene. Wide eyes, wild faces. Hare and Burke, standing, crouched, staring at Robbie. A chair on its back.

151

Someone—a woman—lying on the floor, shoeless, yellowed feet and toenails hooked like a bird's talons, hairy twisted legs exposed, skirts rucked up from a struggle, head covered by the gray pillow that Burke held forced to her face. Arms outstretched, crucified, the hands in claws. A whisky bottle on the floor, knocked over, its contents soaking into the wood. Burke's jacket pulled off his shoulders. Hare's face etched with long red scratches.

Robbie knew then. Knew what he should have known all along. Knew why the bodies were so fresh.

A frozen moment. But then smashed into action. Hare got to the door before Burke, but Robbie was halfway down the stairs, clearing them in two leaps. He ran from the house, followed at snapping distance by the two men.

Blindly running. Unbreathing panic. Robbie faster, younger, gaining ground. People leaping aside. Angry noises. Shouting from the chasing men, "Thief! Stop the thief!" A man trying to trip Robbie but Robbie leaping aside, as though carried by the wind.

Homeward. Could he reach it? But no—they would see where he lived. Where else to go? No time for choices. He simply ran, flew, sliding round corners. Sometimes left, sometimes right. Doubling back, a random route. Anything to shake them off. Suddenly he fell, tripping over a loose stone, but he was flying so fast, so smoothly, that he simply rolled, almost somersaulting in the air, landing on his feet and running as if nothing had happened, as if nothing could ever stop him.

A narrow passage. Robbie ran into it. Steps, a long steep flight of steps, slippery with grime. Robbie stumbled down them, three, four, five at a time, one hand grabbing a flimsy wooden rail. A curse as one of the men tripped behind him.

152

But still the gasping, the shouting, the pursuing footsteps. Robbie leapt the final flight and took the corner sharply.

Uphill now, heading into the sun. The castle swayed over him, as if it must surely topple. Still, he ran. His tongue stuck dry to the roof of his mouth. A pain in his side now. And in his hand. Empty weakening legs. His breath in tightened gasps. He must not stop.

Footsteps still behind him.

He slowed to swing round another corner. As he turned, he glimpsed their snarling faces. Saw the thick club in Hare's hand. They were closer. How could they still be there? Would they never tire? He could hear their labored breathing, imagine Hare's evil spittle on his neck. They were going to catch him. Any moment now. The air like knives inside his chest.

It happened in an instant. As he swung round another corner. In front of him. A man, old, holding a pistol. His startled oyster-pale eyes. Robbie dodging, twisting. Slipping. Falling. A sickening rip in his bandaged hand. A crack as his head hit the wall. Black.

Into the storm roared endless noise and crashing stars and rushing black water. He had no feet. Hands huge. He was everywhere. Black again. Then jumbled shouting. Tongue fumbling. Tunnel swimming. Up downing. Drowning.

His mother floated by. Waving. Smiling. He dived to reach her but their fingers, miles long, stretched and stretched and stretched until they were only lines that went forever toward a point they could never reach. He called to her. She smiled back. She beckoned with a finger. He tried to go toward her, but his legs spindled in the air and she drifted further and further away. "Come back!" he tried to call, but heard only a moaning wind disappearing into never.

He tumbled into waking and found himself groaning. His head throbbed. Two faces swam above his head. No, one face. An old man, his wispy white hair like fog around his ghost-thin skin.

Quickly, Robbie realized where he was. Lying on the street where he had fallen, a crashing pain in his head. Hare and Burke nowhere to be seen.

"Are ye hurt, laddie?" The pistol was steady in the man's frail-looking hand.

Robbie got to his feet with difficulty, leaning his left hand heavily against the wall. His eyes swimming. His head thick thunder. He looked down at his bandaged hand, now dirty and wet. Blood spreading through the dirt.

"No. I'll . . . I know a doctor." Almost. He had to find Joseph as quickly as possible. He felt his head, moving his fingers carefully through his hair. Found the swelling. He winced. Looked at his fingers. No blood.

"Who was chasing you, laddie?" The man waved his pistol.

"I don't know. Thieves? I don't remember."

"Aye, well, this soon frightened them off. I'll wager they thought they'd get the better o' me without it. There's no powder in it, o' course. Cannae keep it dry." His quavery laugh fluttered. "I've killed Frenchmen wi' more courage than them."

Robbie leant against the wall, waiting for his strength to return. The old man sucked air through toothless gums. "The revolution, laddie, the revolution. I was there, at the barricades, helping the poor people o' France. And where did it get them? Deed, that's where. Aye, and then when a few brave Scotsmen tried to rise and fight agin their country's own injustice, where did it get them? Eh? Hanged. Hanged or transported. Hanged or transported." Spittle flew from the man's mouth as his eyes blazed. "And now look at us, look at our city. It's nae more than a midden. And what are we doing? What are ye young people doing about it? Why d'ye no' fight agin it? Agin the injustice?" A tear gathered in one pink-rimmed eye. He stabbed the air with his pistol, before tucking it into his belt.

Robbie's hand was hurting properly now. He rocked it against his chest. He shook his head. The bandage was almost completely red. He needed to go. "I'm sorry," he said. "I need to . . . my hand."

"Aye, laddie, off ye go." And the old man shook his head and tottered slowly on his way, muttering and shaking his fist against the world.

"Thank you, sir," called Robbie after him, before hurrying toward the street where Joseph lived. He kept watching for Burke and Hare, but there was no sign of them. As he neared the end of Fleshmarket Close, he heard his name. "Robbie!" It was Essie. He looked up. She was hanging out of the window. A few moments later she was running toward him, saw the blood immediately.

"Your hand! You need a doctor."

"I'm going to Joseph."

"No! No' Joseph! A proper doctor!"

"Essie, he can do it just as well. And he's closer. By the time I found another doctor, it would be worse."

"So I'm coming wi' you." And she marched in front of him, hurrying him. He shivered in the cooling air and the blood from his hand dripped onto the ground. Soon they turned into the archway that led into Joseph's close. Drying clothes swung high above them, like seagulls. The wind washed through the close from north to south, carrying away some of the stench.

They began to climb the stairs.

Somewhere in the distance a violin sang, rising and falling, its gentle arpeggios rocking like a lullaby. It was a long time since Robbie had heard a violin played like that, like the song a swan might sing. Its sad sound glided, hovering in the twilight.

The sound grew closer as they approached Joseph's floor. Robbie stopped. It was coming from Joseph's door. But Joseph had said he did not play the violin. And in that same moment, Robbie realized. He stepped back, away from the door. Turned to go down the stairs.

"Where're you going?" said Essie.

"There's someone with him. I can't go in."

"Aye, you can. You're a muckle great fool. Look at the blood. You'll die if you don' go in." Essie stretched up to the heavy iron knocker and let it crash three times. The violin stopped. The door opened. Joseph came out, surprised. "What is it, Essie? Robbie?"

Robbie was leaning against the wall, the blood drained from his face. Joseph moved quickly toward him. "What have you done? You will need to come in." Robbie had no choice. He allowed himself to be led inside the room, followed by Essie.

Dr. Robert Knox stood with his back to the fire, the yellow violin under his chin giving his face a buttered glow. The bow rested in his right hand, the fingers curled delicately around, the little finger hovering like mist. He lowered the instrument when he saw them come into the room. Laid it gently on the table. He brushed some specks of rosin from the sleeve of his shirt, the lacy cuffs flapping. A jeweled brooch spangled on his throat and several golden chains hung in perfectly spaced arcs. Near him across a chairback lay his coat, wine-dark in the firelight. The floral perfume bloomed in the warmth of the room.

Joseph was talking. "This is Robbie, Dr. Knox. He—"

"We have had the pleasure already." Dr. Knox bowed. Essie and Joseph looked surprised. Robbie's heart thumped hard. "Robbie was interested in this." Knox gestured to the violin lying on the table, shining softly. "My friends thought he was intending to steal it. He meant no harm." He turned to Robbie. "I did not know you were acquainted with my best student, laddie." His eyes, black against the firelight, held Robbie's gaze, and his mouth twisted in a small sardonic smile.

Robbie dared to breathe.

Joseph spoke. "He has cut his hand quite deeply and I have already repaired it, but he appears to have damaged it again."

"No doubt the result of your unpracticed handiwork, young man," said Dr. Knox, his voice still lightly smiling. "Never trust a man whose face is so perfectly formed, Robbie. It is a face that has not learnt the lessons of life." Joseph bowed slightly, at ease in Knox's presence. Knox walked toward Robbie. Pulled out a chair. Gestured for him to sit. Robbie obeyed. He looked down.

"Put your hand on the table, laddie." Knox rolled his white sleeves back, tucked the lace away. Robbie watched the pumice-stone forehead, the dark dusty hair swept back in ridges. The thick volcanic skin. Knox began to unwrap the wet bandage carefully. Joseph opened his bag and brought out fresh bandages. Curved needles. Steel scissors. Other

157

metal tools of different shapes. A brown glass jar with a cork gummed with something black. He put a bowl of water on the table. Its steam danced slowly upward.

The surgeon's scent drifted over Robbie's face, into his nose. His thoughts raced. This man, with his breath so close, this was the man who bought the bodies of murder victims. Did he know that people were dying in order for him to practice his godless art? Surely he could not know. He must surely believe they were hanged criminals. As Robbie had believed.

Someone must stop the murders. Who else but Robbie could do it? And how could he? The only way was to inform Dr. Knox that the bodies he bought were innocent murder victims. Then, surely, Knox would act. Surely. Would he not? But what if Knox already knew about the murders? Then Robbie would be entirely in his power.

Yet Robbie had to act. There was no one else. He had to do something right. Otherwise how could he live with himself? How could he move forward as he wanted? For himself and Essie. His mouth was dry. He felt paralyzed in this man's presence.

Joseph was lighting three oil lamps. He placed them on the table where Knox sat facing Robbie. Eels of inky smoke swam toward the ceiling. In the sallow glow, Robbie could see the one flaccid eye, the one piercing one.

Essie had been standing silent during this time. She looked from Joseph, to Knox, to Robbie, as if wondering what they all were to each other. Suddenly she spoke. "I've seen you somewhere afore," she said to Knox, boldly. Robbie's heart beat faster. The Flodden Wall! She was there. She must not say it! Please let Essie not say it.

"No doubt you have. Edinburgh is a small place. I am

quite often to be seen." Knox did not look up from what he was doing. His legato voice was soothing.

"But—"

Robbie spoke quickly. "Essie, you should go. I'll see you at home. Buy us some food. Make some of your broth."

"We've nae money left."

Joseph took a coin from his pocket. Essie looked away. "I wan' tae stay."

"No, Essie. Go!" Robbie snapped staccato words. He did not want her here. Did not want Joseph here either. Did not want anyone to hear what he had to say.

"The little girl should go," said Knox. Essie's spell did not work on him. To him, she was perhaps nothing more than a scraggy child with a dirty face and clouded, hostile eyes. "Joseph, would you take her? I cannot work with a child watching me." Essie bristled, her skinny fists clenching, but Robbie met her eyes with a glare and she followed Joseph out, her bare feet slapping the floorboards. The door closed behind them and Robbie was alone with Dr. Knox.

Knox's fingers, long and spiderlike, continued to ease the bandage away, while pressing hard on Robbie's wrist. The bandage became cleaner, redder. Robbie squeezed his eyes shut. Knox could do anything now, had him utterly in his power. Into his head flashed the sickening image of those three knives. But he had to speak.

He opened his eyes again. "There is something I must tell you." The words spurted out. "About the . . . bodies you dissect." Robbie stopped and took some breaths, his vision swarming. "The bodies you think are from the gallows? The bodies you buy?" he added when Knox said nothing. A hesitation before Knox removed another layer of bandage, while keeping pressure on the wrist.

159

Robbie continued. "They're not . . . they're not from the gallows. They're murdered. The men . . . aaagh!" A sudden shooting pain. He looked down. The bandage had come away and the edges of the wound were ragged, with blood welling from deep within. Brown strings curled from the edges.

"Look away," ordered Knox. Robbie turned and continued, through the pain that sliced his breath away as Knox worked. "The men . . . you buy . . . the bodies . . . from . . ." Robbie fought to push away the dusk that smurred across his eyes. "They kill them. They killed a woman today . . . I saw her."

A pause, long and still, poised. The pain less now, dull. A pressing inside. "You saw them kill this woman?"

"Yes!"

"You actually saw them kill her?"

"I saw . . . no, but I know . . ."

"You know nothing. You saw nothing. Nothing but a dead criminal."

"But I know . . ."

"You know nothing, I said!" snapped Knox, his living eye sharp. "I buy the bodies of hanged criminals. It is permitted. Close your eyes." He continued to work on Robbie's hand. Robbie could feel tugging, dully unpleasant, nothing more.

"If it is allowed," said Robbie, "why is it so secret? Why is it done in the middle of the night?" He could no longer feel what Knox was doing.

Knox paused before answering, his voice cello sounding soft as plums. "Because I buy more bodies than the law allows. That is all. I need them. I need them for my work, work that saves lives. Your life, perhaps. Everyone knows what I do. Everyone knows of my skill. People may not like the idea of anatomy but they all too quickly forget their qualms when I save their lives."

"Don't you mind where the bodies come from? Don't you mind who they were?"

Robbie thought of the innocent victims stuffed into herring barrels. And the one he had helped carry down the stairs, its neck bones snapping under his hands. His stomach turned over at the thought. How could this man not mind?

"Why should I mind? Look at your hand." Robbie looked. His hand and wrist were crusted and smeared with dried blood. But from the cut, at least three inches long, sewn together by yellowy-brown thread, not a drop of blood oozed. "I stopped the blood vessel inside your wrist. Joseph had stitched the edges of the wound, with admirable competence—though no more than one would expect from a pupil of mine—but this time it was not enough. I, however, have stopped the bleeding. So, do you mind whose body I was cutting into when I discovered new facts about the anatomy of the blood vessels of the hand and arm? Do you mind whose body I cut into to learn what I needed to save your life? For save your life I have. You would have bled until you died, without my skill."

"I mind when someone dies for you to learn these facts." Anger made Robbie bold.

"You do not know that. I told you—you saw nothing. You saw nothing."

Robbie was not reaching this man. He might as well have stood at the foot of the castle and beat his hands against the rock. "I am not talking about that."

Knox said nothing. Gently he wiped the blood from Robbie's arm with a cloth soaked in warm water from the bowl.

161

"I am not talking about that," repeated Robbie after a moment to take his breath. To prepare for what he was going to say.

"I assume you are going to tell me what you are talking about?"

"My mother died."

Knox's face remained unmoved as he wound a new bandage tightly around Robbie's hand. Robbie stared deep, ugly deep, into Knox's face. Into the living eye like coal. Into the dead eye like pig fat. Felt himself outside that cold closed door again, listening, rocking, rocking, rocking. He continued.

"She had an operation. She screamed in pain. I heard her. I was only a child. I was outside the room. She died screaming, five days later."

"It happens. It happens often. I do not know why it happens some times and not others."

Robbie knew what he wanted to say. It shrieked through his body. But somehow, he could not say it. Could not say, "You were the surgeon. You were the man who killed her. Do you not even remember?" A stupid heat swam behind his eyes. If he had spoken, he would have cried.

He could not reach this man with his heart of rock. Could only hate him.

Knox stood up. "I have finished. Your hand will heal. Keep the bandage on for four days. It is well known that air contains poison. Rest, eat little. If you have a fever, go to the dispensary. Cupping will cure fever. Or go to Joseph if you are concerned. He has been well taught but he requires practice and will likely not charge you."

Robbie's good hand flew to his pocket. Money! He would need to pay Knox. Yet he had none. Knox waved his arm dismissively. "It is nothing. I am a guest in Joseph's home. You are a friend of his. I would not take money from you."

Now Robbie was even further in the man's debt. He recoiled at the thought. He needed to hate him, not feel grateful to him. Again.

He had to ask. "Why did you have me freed before?"

Knox looked at him. "I have no idea what you are talking about."

"When I was thrown in the Canongate Tollbooth. After Professor Syme caught me—in Surgeons' Hall. You had me released."

That musical laugh again, the head thrown back. The sound that had curdled Robbie's blood a few weeks ago on a darkening street. "That was you? I had no idea! It did not concern you. It concerned only me and Syme. Anything Syme wants, I fight against. I cannot abide the man! Boring, pompous, arrogant—I could go on." When he laughed, his face moved thickly like leather pocked by mildew. Robbie spat inside. It was when Knox laughed that he could hate him most.

So, thought Robbie furiously, Knox had only had him freed because of hatred of another man? Was he himself worth nothing in this man's eyes?

Knox straightened his clothes, flicked away a fleck of something on his trousers, tugged his cravat and smoothed the perfect points of his collar. He twirled the edges of his side-whiskers. "I believe you have a home to go to, young man." Still smiling, he clicked his heels together sharply and bowed to Robbie, one arm swirling through the air toward the ground. The lacy cuff danced as his wrist curled, and his fingers spiraled.

Robbie walked toward the door, turned, forced himself to express his thanks. As he walked out, the perfume followed him and hatred welled inside him, as natural as blood. Hatred for the man who had saved his life.

As he walked the short distance home, through a freshening breeze, leaving that scent, that face, behind him, he knew one thing for certain. It was hatred of this man that had almost destroyed him before. For his own good, and for Essie's, he must never see Knox again. Must clean him from his mind completely. The thought of his fingers touching him, his corpse-skinned face looming over him . . . No! He must move forward and wipe the man away, leaving him like a trail of dirty footprints behind him. He had done what he could to stop the murders. He had spoken out, told the truth. Now, if Burke and Hare—and Knox—wanted to hang themselves, how could he stop them? And why should he try? All he could do was have nothing more to do with any of them.

He walked away and left Knox's face behind him.

That night, his sleep was long and deep. But somewhere deeper, a tiny flicker of something not quite known. Far away in his sleeping mind, spinning upward. What was it? The truth? That it was not enough? That there was something more that he should have done? But he was asleep. It wisped away.

He woke in the morning, clearheaded. Out of the window the crystal air rippled around an early buttermilk sun. Move forward. Shut the past away. Stamp quickly on any darker thoughts.

He would throw himself into his studies again. He would

make something of himself. Something that would make Essie happy. Go to university, as Joseph had suggested. He would push away the thoughts of Knox and what was happening in another street.

He would need work. "I'll find work too!" said Essie, mixing some weevily flour with the last of yesterday's milk and spooning it sizzling onto the girdle hanging over the fire.

"Oh, and where will you find someone who will pay you?" he teased.

"Easy. And I'll wager I'll find work afore you!" She flipped the sizzling pancake with a bannock spade and a few seconds later she picked it up with her fingers and tossed it from hand to hand until it cooled enough to eat. Robbie thought she would never outgrow her pleasure in food. Faintly, the magpie sparkle was returning. It was like a star that, when you look straight at it, is not there, but when you look away it twinkles at you, teasing.

A few minutes later, she left the room, crumbs still on her lips. "I'll have work afore you, Robbie!" and she danced out of the door. "Nothing dangerous, Essie!" he shouted as she ran down the stairs.

Where could he start? He was not as confident as Essie about finding work. But perhaps Mr. Brown was tired of the crusty-lipped boy who had taken Robbie's place. Perhaps he could have his job back? It was a good place to begin. He set off toward the bakery, toward Arthur's Seat. He could smell the salty seagull tang already. Taste the yeast from the bakery and the hops from the brewery.

To avoid going anywhere near the Flodden Wall, he wove his way through other streets. Past stalls selling fish, the cobbles slithery with cod heads and scales and smashed oysters, shops touting buttons and silk, ostrich feathers dyed

165

every shade of pink and blue, perfume in thick glass bottles with silver stoppers. Past a bookshop, where a large notice in the window proclaimed a new work by Mr. Walter Scott. *The Fair Maid of Perth*, read Robbie as he passed. He could not read the author's name without thinking of the king's visit six years before. And he did not want to think about it. He must move forward.

In the next . . . Robbie stopped. How could he move forward now? He had not passed this window for a long time. And now, his eye was drawn, pulled by something he loved, whether from the past or the present. How could he not look?

Violins. Violins everywhere, their mottled yellow varnish bright in the sunlight. In the window, the instruments were ranged perfectly, hanging from hooks, neatly spaced. They were of different sizes, from the tiniest almost toylike versions to their elegant full-sized cousins. Bows, too, their gentle parallel curves ranged along a wall beside the window. His face pressed against the glass, Robbie could see, on a table further into the shop, the jumbled paraphernalia of creation. Strings and bridges and pegs and half-carved scrolls—Robbie knew them all. Could feel them in his hands.

He went in. A bell jangled somewhere and a round bespectacled man came out from a door at the back. Robbie remembered him. He looked flustered, annoyed. He wiped his hands on an apron smeared with yellow and orange and brown.

"Aye, what d'ye want, lad?"

"I . . . I just want to look."

"I know your sort, lad. You cannae fool me. It's thieving ye'll be after, no' looking. Now, be off wi' ye."

Robbie looked around the room. In contrast to the

166

window display, the inside of the shop was confusion. A cacophony. Shelves on the back wall hung open, their labels flaking. Strings spiraled on the floor like hairs in a wigmaker's. Through a doorway into the back, Robbie could see sawdust and shavings on the floor, a workbench with a violin mold held in a clamp, slivers of wood, shelves with bottles of varnish, their sides stained every shade of brown, red and yellow.

"Be off wi' ye, I said. Before I throw ye out."

"Please, sir," said Robbie, with all the gentle politeness he could find, "I am not a thief. I was only looking. When I was younger, I had a violin from this shop."

The man peered at him through tiny wire spectacles halfway down his nose. "You would like to buy a violin? Ye'll no' mind if I say . . ."

"No, I have no money. I am looking for work. I am studying to go to university." The words came out suddenly, without planning.

The man pushed his spectacles up his nose. There was a smear of white powder on his shoulder. One wing of his black coat collar stuck up, trapped by the string of his apron. He wore a white cravat, its wrinkled ridges lopsided. The flesh of his neck was loose, chickeny, and his remaining hair sat around the back of his head like a white crescent moon. He looked at Robbie, weighing him up. Robbie kept his bandaged hand behind his back.

"I can tidy your shop for you. I can run errands. And I can read and write, do arithmetic. I can look after your shop while you work on your violins. Stradivarius models, are they not?"

It was that which persuaded the man to take Robbie on.

"I cannae pay ye very much," he warned, "but if ye work

167

hard, show me I can trust ye . . . Aye, I'll gie ye a chance. My name is Mr. Blair."

Robbie had found himself a job. And as he spent the morning sweeping, tidying, sorting, he smiled at the thought of Essie's face. He breathed in the rosin dryness, the heady varnish smell of the shop. Each time he picked up a violin, as his hand cupped the scroll, the perfect-seeming spiral at the end, he wanted to hold it to his cheek and once or twice he did so, when he knew Mr. Blair was not looking, and closed his eyes and smelt his mother.

His hand did not throb at all. By the time Mr. Blair had noticed the bandage, Robbie had transformed the appearance of the shop. He could not question Robbie's ability to help him. And the boy spoke well, as though educated.

Mr. Blair even told him the secret of the Stradivarius scroll, the perfect God-given mathematics that made the twist curl round and round and round, in perfectly reducing spirals, to an endless place that could only be imagined. Like a shell, he said, made by God. If you try to copy it by art, you will fail. Only with perfect mathematics can you achieve the perfect shape and the perfect sound. The golden mean, this mathematical miracle was called. Robbie listened and watched, transfixed.

At the end of the day, Robbie said goodbye to Mr. Blair. He left the shop, with smears of varnish on his hands from the untidy bottles. Their names rolled around his head: gamboge, oak pigment, yellow ochre and, best of all, the fiery orange of dragon's blood. He walked west toward home, with the late afternoon sun warming his face. Essie was there first, her face shining.

"I got work afore you! I telt you I would."

"Well done, Essie! But it is 'told,' not 'telt.' And I'll not be long behind you. I'll have a job tomorrow." He had no desire to take away all her pleasure.

"So, are you no' going to ask what it is?"

"Tell me, then, Essie. What job did you find?"

"Mr. Brown, Robbie! He gave me your old job! I telt—told—him about your hand an' he said you can work for him again when you're all better!"

Essie was almost dancing with excitement and pride. God was looking after them, just as she always believed He would.

Robbie threw himself into this new life, blocking out anything else. He kept well away from Hare's inn and Burke's house. More than once he saw a woman he remembered from the inn, but she passed by and did not notice him. Perhaps did not recognize him, now that he was clean and upright and clear-eyed. His jaw, too, was more square. There were shadows that had not been there. No longer a boy.

His hand healed easily. After a few days, it was itching unbearably and he took the bandage off, though Knox had told him not to. The edges of the cut had knitted together and there was no oozing, though the whole hand was white and wrinkled with dampness from the now dirty bandage. He left the bandage off and very soon the air had dried the cut and he was left with a thin scar that faded daily.

"You'll want your job back," said Essie, hesitantly, when she saw how his hand had healed. But he was happy to let her keep the job. He was content amongst his violins.

May melded into June, the summer days hazy. Ladies sweated in their long dresses and layers of petticoats. Robbie and Essie went barefoot every day now. Robbie's hair was too long, sticking in his eyes, so he borrowed a sharp knife from one of the women in the flesh market and cut it as neatly as he could.

Midsummer Day, eye-squintingly hot. Mr. Blair let him finish early and he walked out onto the humming streets. He looked up. The blue swam away forever. A gull wheeled, little more than a tiny tick in the distance. Arthur's Seat danced in the faraway heat. An idea came to him. How Essie would like it! He hurried to their home to fetch what he needed, and then to the bakery, to catch her before she left. On the way, he stopped at a market stall. He put his purchase in his pocket, wrapped in several layers of old paper.

Mr. Brown looked up when Robbie arrived through the door. His face split into a broad smile. "Rabbie! Is it Essie ye're aifter? She'll be here in a wee bit."

"Guid afternoon, Mr. Brown. Aye, I came fo' Essie. Will she be ready fo' hame soon?"

"Aye, she will so, Rabbie. A richt guid worker she is. Not that ye'd ken it, fae looking at they skinny arms." Mr. Brown wiped his hands on his apron and swept some pieces of warm oat farl into a twist of paper, which he gave to Robbie. The heat spread through the paper.

"Thank ye, sir!" said Robbie. He helped Mr. Brown tidy up, sweeping the flour and crumbs and dried mud from people's feet out of the door.

There was Essie. Cochineal-cheeked in the heat. Her face lit up when she saw Robbie. They said goodbye to Mr. Brown.

"This way, Ess," said Robbie, turning the other way, away

from the town and away from home, toward Salisbury Crags and Arthur's Seat.

"Where are we going?" she asked.

"You'll see soon enough."

They stopped to drink at a public well and went on. Past the grazing sheep. Past the railway workers, brown muscles glistening as they hefted huge rocks onto horse-drawn wagons with levers and ropes. The tunnel entrance seemed deeper, darker each time Robbie came this way, blasted by regular powder charges. Essie waved at the men and they waved back. They were used to seeing her, with her bread barrow.

"Where are we going?" asked Essie again.

"I told you—you will see soon enough."

Further along the track, they came to the loch. Robbie turned away from the path, toward the steep slopes on the left. Together they climbed through the heather, scrambling over stones. Away from the people. Away from all the noise and smell and taste of the city.

Higher they climbed, until the people were ants below them. Breathless, they lay down, the grass beneath them springy, softer than any mattress they could imagine. On their stomachs they lay, chins on hands, staring at the city to the west. A visitor could only marvel at the dramatic silhouette. From here, outside, they could almost forget its real character. It was like a royal portrait, showing only what the sitter wants to reveal.

The sun was sinking, but slowly, and on this longest day of the year it would cling on for as long as possible. The evening rays were still hot, and the hours of lightness stretched ahead.

"I'm hungry," said Essie, her cheeks pinked by the sun and the climb.

"You are always hungry." And he pulled the package from one pocket but did not unwrap it. "First, a fire. We need something for tinder, and sticks."

"What'll we light it with?" asked Essie.

He pulled flints from the other pocket.

"What's the fire fo'?"

"There'll be no fire at all if you witter on. We need sticks, Essie, and grass for tinder." She ran off and within minutes had returned with an armful of dry grass and wood.

She stacked it expertly and he struck the flint again and again until one spark and then another jumped into the grass. Shielding it with her hands, Essie softly blew and they watched the tiny flames lick the dry twigs and flare up. More sticks, and soon a good blaze was going. "Now, stones," said Robbie, and he searched until he found two flat stones. He put them in the fire and piled more sticks on top.

"What now?" asked Essie.

"Now, you wait," he replied.

She stared at the flames, the firelight bright in her eyes. They were silent in their own thoughts. Robbie lay back on the grass and chewed a piece of clover, tasting its sweetness. Essie picked petals off tiny flowers and watched them flutter down into the fire. Eventually, once the flames died down, Robbie unwrapped the package. Her eyes opened wide. Beefsteak! Purple with freshness! It was months since she had had meat like that. Her mouth watered. With a stick they raked the burning wood aside and laid the steaks on the stones. A sizzling sound. And almost immediately the smell of roasting meat. After a minute or two, they turned them with a stick. Smoke stung their eyes and blackened their faces.

They ate the steak with their fingers, red juices running down their chins. Essie laughed and told him he looked like a Highlander.

Afterward, they wiped their hands on the grass. Essie lay back against the cushioning ground and smiled with content. Her stomach full, her skin warm, all fear forgotten. God was watching over them, she knew.

"Thank you, Robbie."

Robbie sat for a while and watched her as she fell asleep, the birdlike movements of her face slowly quietening. Now she looked fragile, her cheeks poppy-red.

Later, as the fallen sun chilled the air, he woke her. Drowsily, she allowed him to help her up and lead her down the slope again. They walked slowly back into the town, and came to Fleshmarket Close in near darkness, the smell of the smoke hanging in their clothes.

The weeks, months, passed. Summer swelled, bloomed, pulsed with mist. Flies swarmed amongst the filth of the streets, and the stench blossomed, but in the distance, if Robbie looked high enough, far enough, the days stretched into a hazy blue somewhere, where the bees swam sleepily and the heather blushed on the faraway dancing hills.

It was almost possible to imagine that this was how it would always be. Moving forward, moving upward, as though all the darkness was left behind forever.

9

Discovery

Soon summer was past and autumn's fingers had crept into the cockroach darkness. A chill draft rattled the windows and blew across the table as Robbie worked at his books late one evening, while Essie slept. The candle flickered, sizzled, and went out, drowned in its own liquid. He moved to relight it and as he passed the window, he happened to look out. It was the moon that he looked at first, its huge perfect globe hanging as if by magic. By its light, he could see the twisted cliffs of leaning tenements and the tiny houses crumpled between them. He looked down.

It was then that he saw it. Out of the corner of his eye, movement. A cart. The familiar shape of a herring barrel rocking under its ropes. Trundling fast. Pulled by two men. His throat contracted and he shrank back from the window. Sat down, breathing fast. Sick. He knew who it was. What it was. There had been another murder.

It was then that he realized, suddenly, something that deep down in that deepest darkest part of his mind he had known all along. Something he had tried to shut out. He had tried to hide from it by burying himself in his studies, in the rosin-dusted haven of the violin shop, in his tidy routine life of the last few months. He must stop the murders. There was no one else. Meanwhile there had been another victim. He had not done enough. This time it was his fault.

As he climbed into bed later that night, carefully so as not to wake Essie, he knew what he would have to do. He would have to report Burke and Hare to the authorities.

How? If the constables went to Burke's house, they would find nothing. Nothing but a pile of straw and a dirty pillow. And Burke and Hare would know they were under suspicion. Perhaps that alone would be enough to stop them? No. They would find somewhere else to do it. They were too greedy to stop. And they would certainly come searching for Robbie.

There was only one way. Robbie would have to wait until they were about to do it again. He would have to watch the house. Every day until he saw them bringing a new victim to their murder house. He felt cold at the thought. He did not want to see their faces again, to be reminded of what he had done. Or to think of Knox buying the bodies, sallow in the gaslight.

The next morning he told Mr. Blair that his sister was ill. He needed to be with her until she was better—if she was ever better, he said. Mr. Blair's kindly watery-blinking concern when Robbie told him about Essie made him feel guilty. But it was the only way.

Ten days it took. Ten days during which Robbie haunted the Canongate, taking every opportunity to pass the house where Burke lived, always with his collar pulled up, always holding his breath as he walked past. The tattered winds of autumn whipped his cheeks. Icy rain dripped down his neck. Each morning, the daylight shriveled a little more, the darkness creeping in as if a tombstone was slowly sliding over the city. Several times he saw Burke, always walking carefree, smiling greetings to someone he knew, or touching his hat when a lady passed, or lashing out with his foot at a dog. Sometimes from across the street Robbie even saw his freckled skin, the wet pale eyes.

Once he saw Hare with him, walking toward Burke's house. His heart tripped. This was it! But no—there was no one with them and they came out again immediately.

At last, inevitably, the moment came. Robbie was some yards away when he saw them, walking toward the house. With another man, stooped, slow, tottering. An old beggar, chewing, weighed down by his brown layers of cloth. Hare led the way, his eyes darting round, his wet mouth open. Robbie shrank round a corner, peered back. Burke's hand was on the beggar's shoulder, pushing him along. He smiled down at the man, agreeing with some rambled comment, soothing. Robbie's skin contracted. Hare fumbled at the door; it opened; they led the man in. Robbie's last sight was Burke's milky eyes looking out into the street before the door closed.

Robbie ran. Toward the Canongate Tollbooth. He needed a constable. Quick, before it was too late! Or a soldier would do. There! But he could not do it himself. Too dangerous. He would be questioned and remembered. He looked around. A boy kicked stones nearby, oblivious to the cold. Robbie, head turned away from the soldier a few yards away, walked up to the boy. "See this coin, lad?" The boy's eyes were fixed on the coin as Robbie twirled it in front of him. The boy tried to snatch it but Robbie was too quick and held it high. "You would like to earn this coin, would you not?" The boy nodded, staring at it. "Now, listen carefully. You see that soldier?" The boy nodded again. "Now look down the street, two houses past where that gray horse is standing, the low house with the sagging roof? Now, you go to that soldier and you tell him—and listen carefully," and at this Robbie put his face close to the boy's face, "you tell him that in that house there's a murder happening." The boy's eyes opened wide. He swallowed. "You understand?" urged Robbie. The child nodded and held out his hand. Robbie placed the coin in the small palm and the boy started to move away. Robbie grabbed his wrist. "Not so fast. I haven't finished yet." He took another coin from his pocket. The child stared, his eyes red-rimmed in the cold. "This coin is for you too," he said, "when I see the soldier going into that house. Now go! Hurry!"

The child ran, barefoot in the cold, and Robbie watched from round a corner while the boy talked to the soldier. The soldier did not seem to listen. He seemed to laugh, and turn away. Robbie's heart raced. The boy persisted and the soldier called another soldier from inside the Tollbooth. The two of them looked at each other, spoke again to the boy, and then moved quickly down the street toward Burke's house. Robbie held his breath as they knocked at the door, waited, knocked again, and then hurled their shoulders at the heavy door.

The boy was running toward him. Robbie threw the coin at his feet and ran away himself.

Home. Light-footed he sped, the weight falling from him. He could have sung as he ran up the stairs. Could have danced with relief. It was done! No more murders. Now justice.

The feeling of relief did not last long. What about the man? The beggar who had followed Burke and Hare, trusting, unknowing. Had the soldiers reached him in time? Or had Robbie watched the man walk to his own death? Robbie had set a trap and the bait was an innocent beggar. Had he cared enough about the new victim? Did this not make him just as bad as Knox, who believed that it did not matter how he obtained bodies if his purpose, his motive, was for the benefit of medicine?

But no! He could not think like this. If this beggar had indeed become the latest murder victim, there was nothing else Robbie could have done to stop it. His whole aim had been to stop any more murders happening. And to bring the murderers to justice. There was no other way he could have achieved that. Now Hare and Burke would hang. Maybe Knox, too. At the thought, Robbie stopped. What was it Hare had said? "We hang, you hang." They would not do it. Surely they would not? Besides, they would have no idea that it was Robbie who had reported them. It could have been anyone. And who would listen to them anyway?

Trying to reassure himself in this way, he waited for something to happen, for news of their arrest.

He did not have to wait long. The next day. The noises of the street floating upward, distant-sounding, muffled. His skin cold with sweat. He went to the window and looked down. Was there something different? Something buzzing, something shocked about the way the people met and bent toward each other and parted and met someone else? Was that what rumor looked like? A whispering game.

He looked up. The air still and thick. Cold and heavy-looking. Then snow, floating flecks of snow, the first snow of winter. He shivered.

Then he heard it. Spun round. Footsteps, running up the

stairs. The door flying open. Essie. Her cheeks red from the cold. Her eyes wide. Her hair wind-wild.

Her voice was spiky, frightened. "Two men've been arrested, Robbie. For murder. They selt the bodies. An' d'you ken who tae, Robbie?" Her eyes flamed. Her arms were taut by her sides. Robbie said nothing, his words trapped. "Dr. Robert Knox!" She spat the words out. "I said I'd seen him afore. An' I ken just what was on that barrow! It's murder, Robbie! You'll go tae hell!" She was shouting now, lashing out her anger and her fear.

"I didn't know they were murdered!" he shouted. "You can't imagine I would—"

"I don' believe you!" There were tears in her eyes.

"Believe me, Essie. Before God, I swear I did not know. And when I found out, I tried to stop it."

"I don' believe you."

He felt sick. Shaking all over. Cold with a new fear. Everything was falling to pieces again. How could he have thought it would not?

What if Burke and Hare named him? "We hang, you hang." What would it be like to hang? Robbie had watched a few hangings. Had seen one where it did not work first time. He remembered the angry roar of the crowd when the victim dangled with his legs more than twitching, his whole body in spasm, kicking, silently except for the sawing laugh of the rope as it jerked. Had seen when they cut him down, hacked away the rope from his neck, revived him in water and hanged him again, screaming before he dropped. And afterward the crowd had stoned the hangman, would have killed him if the soldiers had not dragged him away.

He could do nothing but wait.

Essie climbed into their bed fully clothed. Made mute

with fear, she pulled the blanket over her head. It was cold in the room. The fire was dead and damp with spluttered soot. No light came from outside. A gale began to blow, battering the windows and the roof and the door. The candlelight shivered. Shadows crept across the ceiling.

Robbie sat. Waited. He knew Essie was not asleep. He could tell by her rigid silence. He went over to her, knelt down by the bed. "Essie," he whispered, pushing a drift of hair from her forehead.

"Believe me, Ess," he said. "I didn't know. I have done foolish things, but I did not know about the murders. Not until it was too late."

She spoke through tight lips. "You see what happens when you say bad things about God? You shouldn't o' said what you said. Tae Joseph. God is punishing us."

"No, Ess. Look at all the bad things that happened before that. Think about all the people who die, babies, innocent babies. I don't know what the answers are, but I do know it is not so simple."

Essie was silent. Then she spoke, her voice stronger. "God will care for us, Robbie. I know He will. Everybody says so. 'Cept Joseph. Mr. Chalmers said, at Sunday School, 'God is the only father o' the fatherless.' God is our father."

If only it was so simple, thought Robbie in the darkness beside her.

"Robbie? If you swear it's true, that you kent nothing 'bout the murders, I'll believe you," said Essie at last.

"I swear it, Essie."

"Everything will be all right now, will it no'?" And she pushed the blanket back and got up. Robbie nodded, silenced by her bright and desperate faith.

With difficulty, Robbie went about the evening routine,

prepared food, fetched water. But part of him hung in the air, helpless. Later, Essie slept quickly, reassured. Robbie lay awake. Each time he nearly drifted away, a sudden heartbeat would wake him again. The city, too, pulsed with silent wakefulness. Could it ever sleep again? But, somewhere in the deepest part of the night, he must have slept.

In the morning they were woken by rain smattering on the window. The sky was a swirling sea-gray. The clean mint snow had gone. Rain churned the mud.

Inside, water began to seep through the ceiling, and he moved a bucket to catch the drips.

It was Sunday. Essie went off to her Sunday School, cheeks scrubbed in cold water, hair forced beneath the once-white cap. With her gone, Robbie's thoughts darted without control. Panic grew. How should he spend the time before the trial? Go about his normal work? Do everything as usual? Just keep away from Hare's inn and Burke's house.

If only he could have spoken to Joseph. But how could he? Joseph was part of Knox's world. Joseph had cut into dead bodies himself, had admitted it openly. Perhaps Joseph knew as much as Knox? Perhaps he was involved? After all, two students had helped unload the cart. Perhaps Joseph had done that too? Besides, if he did not know, he also did not know of Robbie's involvement. Whatever the case, it was not possible for Robbie to speak to him about it.

When he went outside to get water from the well in the High Street, the streets were clotted with groups of huddled people, their Sunday clothes hurriedly pulled on. People looked over their shoulders, spoke with eager frowns, spat their self-righteous anger into the cold air.

"They're saying sixteen people was killt, mebbe more. Men and women. Bairns, too."

Robbie tried to grasp the enormity of sixteen murders. Into his head again came the sight of that woman's twisted legs, her rag-doll damaged body. Guilt. He would never forget it. He wondered if he could ever be clean of it. Of the bodies he had carried. Of the beggar he had seen walk to his death. Of the money he had earned.

"Aye, an' it's tha' doctor I blame. Cutting intae deed bodies like tha'. It's no' right! No' natural." The man had a growth spreading over his face, cupping his chin and jaw with its grotesque mass.

"Aye, Dr. Knox. He shuid hang wi' Burke an' Hare, so he shuid."

"Aye, an' then they shuid tak' doon his body and cut it up for a' the world tae see. See how he likes it then."

Robbie's hatred of Knox was growing back, sending its bindweed roots to catch him again. The feeling was sleet-cold, and shaking, and full of darkness. Why, whenever he seemed to have put the past behind him, did that name rear up again? He could not shake the man off.

Alongside this hatred lurked the increasing fear that Burke or Hare would name him, drag him with them to the gallows. There seemed no choices anywhere anymore, whichever way he turned.

Desperately, he threw himself into routine. Surviving, working in the violin maker's shop, trying to keep Essie at her books. What else could he do? How else could the days pass before the trial? If he did nothing, time would stand still.

Through all this, Essie's frightened face accused him. How could he reassure her when he could not reassure himself? Often he found her sitting staring into nothing. One day he found the kaleidoscope grimed in dust under the bed. It was broken, its cylinders sliding uselessly past each other, and when he looked through it he saw only a mess of tumbled shards.

Every day that passed was a day nearer the moment when Hare and Burke might name him, calling him to hang with them. Perhaps he deserved it? He was weighed down by events that were heavier than he could measure. The world was not right. Perhaps it could only be right when Hare and Burke were punished, hanging till they were dead. And then, what about Knox? Robbie's jaw clenched. Perhaps it would not be all over until Knox had paid a price? Perhaps Robbie, too, would have to pay. His neck cringed at the thought.

Sometimes, as he walked along a street, he would hear children chanting the new rhyme as they skipped or played their endless clapping games:

"Doon the close and up the stair
But an' ben wi' Burke an' Hare
Burke's the butcher
Hare's the thief
Knox the man who buys the beef!'

It was difficult not to believe that they chanted it at Robbie as he hurried past.

At last, the day of the trial. Twenty-fourth December. The day before Yuleday. In most years, a passing day like any other. Today, crisp, cold, clear, blue. A day drum-tight. A day of brittle fear, light-headed, breathless. He waited. Waited for the word to spread.

Countless times, he went outside the violin shop, looked

up and down the hushed streets, watched the faces of the few people who shivered by. Mr. Blair had begun to teach him how to scrape and shave the wood from the backpiece of a half-made violin. Today, he took no pleasure in the tiny curls that dropped to the ground at his feet. He could not hold the tool steady. He overheated the red-hot bending iron and dropped it on the floor, where a tiny fire blazed up amongst the shavings. Mr. Blair's voice rose in exasperation as he threw water on it.

But it was not until the early hours of the following morning that the word came. The city woke to whispers. Soon the news was everywhere. William Hare had been freed. He had agreed to give all the information that would send his friend to the gallows, in return for his own freedom. William Burke would hang, just over one month from now, and when he was dead he would be taken down and dissected. In public, for all to see. It was only right, everyone said. Only right that his body should be sliced and opened and split and gouged and laid bare to the mob. It was justice, they all said, their eyes bright, sneering in self-righteous disgust.

Knox's name was kicked about in the grime. The evil doctor who had bought the bodies. He must have known, they all said. If he had not known, he should have asked. Robbie's hatred grew on the wind of their anger. It mattered nothing to him that Knox had saved his life; he had forgotten. Or that Knox had freed him from prison; it had been for his own twisted ends, in any case. The hatred was something in Robbie's guts, outside his control. If Knox had asked, had cared, had given a single thought to the living instead of burying his arms in corpses, none of this would have happened. Robbie would not have been tainted and now be in fear of his life.

Knox cared for no one. How could he make Knox care? How could he make him sorry?

But first, the hanging. There was still time for Robbie to be dragged to the gallows himself. Only when Burke was dead could he be sure that the risk had passed.

10

Hanging

Over a month to wait, a month during which Robbie had no time, no space for anything except that date, hanging in the wintered air like icicles. A frozen day mired in the dead darkest reaches of winter. Sickness settled on the city, creeping around the stinking streets, picking off the weakest, the gin-drowsy babies, the young mothers hollow-eyed with disease. Some died of cold, too weak to shiver in their damp rooms, the fires dead in the grates, rain or snow dripping down the chimneys. They slipped away unnoticed, perhaps being discovered days later, rigid. People walked quickly from place to place, hunched against the cold, stiff-shouldered in the wet wind, scarves moist over noses, sweat clotted into frosty side-whiskers.

Beneath all this the city's anger grew, fanned by rumor, by horror at what had been going on unseen in their streets. William Hare was forced to flee for his life. Eventually, word came that he had been seen in an English city, and someone had thrown lime in his eyes, blinding him. Knox's name was still kicked around. The more other doctors and surgeons defended him, the more the mob considered him guilty.

At least Hare was gone. He could not drag Robbie into it

now. Who would listen if he tried? But there was still Burke. What would he have to lose in those last moments before the hangman put the noose around his neck? He could name Robbie and the mob would turn on Robbie.

At last, the hanging day. Robbie woke early, the darkness still deep, a cold wind rattling. Somewhere nearby, a door banging. A baby crying. He lay still, his heart thumping already.

The city buzzed from the early hours.

Essie wanted to watch the hanging. Robbie refused to let her, his face so frosty that she could not argue. She went to her work at the bakery in the early darkness, looking back at Robbie as she left. They had barely talked since the trial, the air between them brittle.

Robbie paced about in the silence. He could not go to work today. He was cold, sweaty, the muscles in his face rigid. He kept looking out of the window, looking for a sign, a sign of anything that he wanted or did not want to hear. It was still dark outside, the northern daylight nowhere near. But he could hear unusual noises and imagine crowds already sweeping toward where the hanging would take place.

There was no air in the room. Robbie could not take a full breath in. Each time he tried, it was as if something sat in his throat.

He had to get out. Pulling on his boots and his jacket and turning the collar up, he left the building, running down the stairs. Once on the High Street, he stood leaning against a building, brushed by the crowds all moving in one direction. The street was clogged with eager people, their faces angry but excited, gray-lipped with cold. Robbie closed his ears to the chatter, the speculation. He breathed in the frosted air.

No one noticed him. He wished he could vanish entirely. Forever.

For a while he stood there, torn. What should he do? Should he join the crowds, be a part of their anger, see justice done? Or should he turn in the opposite direction and run and run and run?

It was almost light now, the sky a scudding charcoal. Robbie clenched his hands, palms sweaty. He pushed himself away from the wall and blended into the crowd, carried along by them. They were the blood in the veins of their city, pulsed along without choosing.

The crowd thickened, slowed. They were nearly at the cobbled square by St. Giles' Cathedral, the heart of the city, where the hanging would take place. He could imagine Burke now, being led, slow with fear, toward the platform with its hanging rope. What was in his head? Just fear? Or anger, too? Would he name Robbie, use his last few moments of life to do what he had promised? "We hang, you hang." Robbie's throat constricted, his breath now as thin as spider silk.

He stopped. Shouts around him, jostling. "What ye doing? Git a move on, will ye?" But he was barely aware of it. He turned and fought his way to the side of the street and pressed himself breathless against a wall again. He could not go on. Could not watch the hanging. How could he have thought he might?

He went the other way. Walked fast. Away from the hanging.

Soon, only stragglers were passing him. The roar of the crowd moved on. Robbie walked faster in his new direction. He did not know where he would go. Perhaps to the Royal Park, Arthur's Seat, anywhere away from here. As he walked faster, his shoulder knocked hard against someone. A woman's voice cried out, "Watch what ye're doing!" Robbie turned briefly to look at her, to mutter his apologies. She looked at him oddly. Did she know him? No, it was just something in his own eyes that disturbed her.

In the pause, he became aware of something. A silence. Utter silence. The city was holding its breath. The woman was still, her face frozen. Their breath clung in the cold air, waiting.

At that moment, they both turned their heads toward the same sound. A roar, a huge surging storm of noise in the distance, a whole city shouting as one. The hanging. It was over. Into Robbie's mind flashed the vision of Burke's body dangling, his legs jerking, his lips hanging open, tongue sticking out. Turning blue. He closed his throat, tightened his stomach. How much pain had Burke felt? Not enough, too quick, nowhere near enough pain.

A spinning feeling in his head. Blackening rain over his eyes.

The woman was speaking, "So, it's o'er. Ye all right, laddie?"

He mumbled something and walked on, slowly at first. It was over. But it did not feel over. Still it did not feel over.

Knox. The hatred was still there. Knox still did not understand the enormity of what he had done. He must be made to know and to care. Knox was the man who was everything that Robbie hated. Still. The man represented pain, and anger, and fear, and failure. He would show Knox what he had done. He would make him understand. He would make him, at the end of it all, be sorry.

Robbie began to hurry again. Soon he was running through almost empty streets. Faster and faster. Toward

Surgeons' Square. Toward Knox's anatomy school. And if Knox was not there he would go to his house. Wherever he was, he would find him. The rain slanted, sleeting into his face, sliding freezing down his neck.

Rounding a corner, he lost his balance, fell hard on the ground. Pain shot through his hip, his breath pumped from his body. He squeezed his face shut against the pain. He had to get up. Covered in mud, he struggled to his feet, put his foot on the ground, tried to put weight on his leg. He winced. It would do. He ran on, limping heavily. His breath rasped in his throat.

"Robbie!" A shout. He ignored it. "Robbie!" He slid to a stop and turned, the rain dripping off his nose and down his chin.

"Go home, Essie! Go home!"

"No! I'm no' going home. I'm coming with you. You'll no' leave me again!"

"You can't come. Go home!" Robbie yelled.

But Essie ran right to him, looking up at him, her hair plastered on her forehead, her eyes blazing through the rain. "I can so! Whatever it is you're going tae do, I'm coming too. You're no' leaving me again."

"No, Essie. Go *home!* This time, you can't come." And he ran, as fast as he could. Faster than Essie could run.

Her anger grew fainter until he could hear it no more. She melded into the pulse of the city.

Round another corner. Infirmary Street. The hospital in front of him. Not far now. He ran faster.

Three men, collars turned up against the rain, hunched shoulders, standing still, their faces sheltered by umbrellas. A conversation, snatched words. The hanging. Was that Knox's name he heard? One man looked toward him, his face wide

191

with recognition. Professor Syme! The man said something. The other two looked up. One old, round, angry-faced even before he saw Robbie. The other—Joseph! Syme began to move toward Robbie. Instinctively, Robbie sprang away. He leapt into the street.

"Robbie!" A shout. He stopped, twisted. "Robbie!" It was Essie, running toward him on the pavement. Suddenly, a clattering. A carriage speeding round the corner. He saw it from the corner of his eye. Saw Essie's silent scream. Hurled himself aside.

Then confusion. The cobbled crashing, metal screeching. Through the squeal of horses, something huge, something hard, hit him and he was flung into the air, landing twisted on his back.

In slow motion, thinly through a veil of pain, he saw a carriage wheel buckle, turn in on itself and fall slowly. And as it fell, and as he lay, he watched the jagged broken spoke slice through the air toward him. As it tore through the flesh and muscle of his shoulder, he was pinned like a fluttering insect to the ground. Then he tumbled down into the blackness and slid away, dropping into nowhere.

Into the nowhere a scream. Shaking him. His own scream, he realized in a blur. Voices all around him, hands touching him, rain on his face. Someone crying.

The pain was paralyzing. He knew it was in his shoulder but every tiniest part of his body was trapped in it. He could not move even a finger. Breathing was difficult. Only shallow breaths. Each a struggle. Not enough air. Blackness. Spreading. Vision. Going to die. Like his mother. God's last word. His punishment.

A splintering sound. His own screaming again, from somewhere that did not feel part of him. Then he was being lifted. On his back he was cradled in many arms and then he felt a rush of wet wind over his face as he was carried away somewhere. He tried to open his eyes but everything was blurred and frightening, upside down and full of strangeness. Every movement was agony.

Then a rattling, more shouting, and he was lowered onto something hard. He floated into the air, lifted again.

Suddenly through the chaos, a voice, strong and sure. "Robbie, it's Joseph. And Essie's here. Try not to move. You chose a good place to have an accident. You are near the Infirmary."

"No!" breathed Robbie. "Not the Infirmary!" But no one seemed to hear.

Through his pain he could hear arguing. Professor Syme's voice. "For God's sake, man! He's nothing but a common thief. Should be dangling from the gallows, not cluttering up our hospitals. Leave him, I say."

Joseph. "I know him, sir. He is not a bad lad."

"Aye, well, what would you know? Did you know he was thrown in prison not so long ago? For stealing? From Surgeons' Hall, would you believe?"

Another voice. "Let the young man deal with this one, Syme, why don't we? See how well he has learnt his lessons."

Robbie felt himself being carried upward, at an angle— steps?—and soon they were indoors. He opened his eyes and through a mist saw marbled columns, lamps everywhere, distant like stars. Suddenly, he came to a halt. A pause. Then, slow, semibreve footsteps, approaching. A shuffling of feet as the men moved aside to let a newcomer near. And then a deep, rich, musical voice.

"What is all this commotion? Causing trouble, are you, Professor Syme? What? Again?" An amused, lyrical tone. The lowest warm tones of a violin.

Through the blackness in front of his eyes, Robbie could not see the man who spoke. But he knew who it was. His heart skittering, pinned like a moth, he looked into Dr. Robert Knox's eyes. This was pure fear. Nothing he had felt before came anywhere near this. If he had had the strength he could have summoned up the anger, too. But what would be the point? He was paralyzed, useless, speared through the shoulder by a piece of wood that was going to kill him.

But Knox only turned to Syme and smiled at him, nose high, eyebrows raised, a delicate tapering finger stroking the side of his chin. A floral scent draped itself over Robbie's face and he breathed it in, wanting to drown in it.

Knox spoke. "My dear Professor Syme, surely you would not turn away this young boy who is so gravely injured? This would not be the mark of a distinguished and virtuous man. But, since you no doubt have a great deal of exceptionally important work to do, I am sure you will allow me to care for this boy. We have met before. I will perform the operation at my own expense, as I so often do. With young Joseph as my able assistant, of course."

Professor Syme, his face purple with anger and unable to look Knox in the eye, turned away with a flick of his hand. "Please yourself, Knox. You always do. No doubt, once he is as dead as your other patients, you will have some use for him." And he walked away, his shoes echoing in the corridor.

Voices swirled around Robbie, snatches of words and sentences, Knox's name several times. A coldness swept through him, numbing his thoughts. Only fear and pain remained. Fear and pain without words. Raw, unbreathing.

He was moving again. As he was carried away, somewhere, he tried to die. Tried to shut everything down, to clamp his heart, to stop breathing entirely.

Through the darkness another voice. Essie. "Robbie! Hush, Robbie. It's going tae be all right." And he felt her warm hand holding his, felt its birdlike lightness. "We're nearly there." No! He tried to squeeze her hand. To tell her that he must not be there, must not go to the Infirmary. But his fingers did not work. He was drifting. Floating toward a place where nothing meant as much as it should.

Along corridors, endless turnings, up stairs, along, around. Now a room, high-ceilinged, wide wet windows. With a searing pain he felt himself being moved onto a table. He did not know if he cried aloud. He was exhausted by the effort of being in pain, of struggling to breathe through ice.

He looked at the ceiling and grew colder. A large spider hung briefly on its thread above him. Watched him watching it. It scuttled back toward the safety of its web. The voices of everyone in the room drifted into the distance. He began to fade, retreat. He could almost believe that this was not going to happen.

He could not hear Essie. Where was she? He began to panic. He tried to move, felt steel hands on his head, his legs, his face, a palm on his forehead, a cloth going over his eyes. His breathing shallowed, quickened, gasping. He was suffocating. It was coming. Whatever it was, it was coming.

Through the fear, that voice. Knox. "Be calm. I have not started yet. Stay very still and very calm. It will soon be over. Breathe slowly and deeply."

The voice barely reached his terror. He wished someone would hit him on the head, knock him out. A pounding in his ears. Every muscle stretched. His head forced into the hard table. His eyes were squeezed shut and the blood danced purple behind them. His legs shook with cold, jerking. He could only wait for what was to come.

The pain was one shattered scream, shooting into a million splinters in his ears. Something was stuffed between his teeth. Every muscle in his body, every joint, jerked into spasm. Something rasping was inside him, scraping against the bones in his shoulder, digging into him, tugging, ripping. He felt blood flow down past his neck and toward his back.

Into space he dived, scrambling away from the fear, scrabbling in the emptiness, struggling to find solid edges to push himself against. But all was vapor beneath him and still fear clung to him. Then, as he tumbled toward cave-cold nothing, suffocating, he saw a glow in the spiraling distance, a misty, growing whiteness. He spun toward it. Fear fell away from him. As if in a dream he flew toward the whitening light, stretched from head to toe on a silver arrow, spiraling unbreathing, silent screaming. As long as he could hold his breath, he would fly toward the light. And he could hold his breath forever, forever and ever and ever. He could stay out here, up here, and never go back. How easy it would be, how dizzyingly easy just to float away.

He watched with detached pity the dwarfed figure of himself pinned on the table in the room below, like a poor damaged butterfly specimen not quite dead.

There was Knox, working fast. He smoothly pulled the wooden spike from Robbie's shoulder and pressed his fingers into the wound to stop the spurting blood. Joseph also had his fingers in the wound, pinching vessels. Between them their hands and knives worked with spiderlike speed and skill and Robbie felt nothing, only watched from afar. Another man held his head, firmly, the hands over his ears.

Robbie floated away, flying higher toward the whiteness. Toward forever. Into his mother's arms.

Robbie smelt her breath on his neck, noticed the sparkle in her angel eyes. She held and held and held him. Together they flew. She did not drop him.

In his head as they spun floated the one question he had wanted to ask. Wanted for so long to ask. "Why did you drop me?" She answered his unspoken question.

"It is simple, Robbie. I had no choice. In some things we just have no choice. In others we do. It is telling the difference that matters. Look down." Robbie looked down, and there was Essie, outside the room. Her hands were over her ears. Her face was screwed tight, her eyes shut, as though by shutting her eyes she could block the sound of Robbie screaming. He moved to go down to her but his mother's voice in his hair whispered, "No! You must not take her with you. She will find her own way."

Floating free in the whiteness, in a place where everything made sense, Robbie understood. He had to finish the journey on his own, as his mother had done.

From somewhere far away, yet somehow deep inside him, came his mother's voice. "You cannot choose what happens to you. But you can choose how to live. You can choose who to be." Still she held him. Until he was ready. Then he let her go.

As she floated away, their fingers parted, slip-sliding, tip-touching, and she was gone, leaving behind the memory of her star-bright eyes. As he drifted alone, he allowed himself another floating moment before returning. Taking a lungful of air, he dived back into the pain and fear.

Controlling his breathing, slow, slow, slow, he hovered somewhere inside himself. His body was a mass of fire, white-hot, as though real flames were eating his skin. He felt his flesh being tugged, pulled, drawn together. Sensed something sharp piercing the skin at intervals. But, strangely, no fear. It was only pain and what was that? He let all his limbs go limp and sank into the table. The cloth had fallen from his face.

Opening his eyes, he saw a man's face above him. The man's hands held his head, but gently now. And there was Joseph, his high cheekbones shadowed in the lamplight, meeting Robbie's wakening eyes. Robbie looked to the left. There was Knox. Concentrating. His one good eye focusing on what he was doing. The other useless eye dead. The pitted face taut. And then a smile. A relaxing. Knox looked at Robbie. "Well done, lad. You will soon be good as before."

Strong hands raised him upright. The pain was dull. His head felt heavy and he let it drop. He let his whole body relax as caring hands bandaged his shoulder tightly, fastening his arm across his chest. Gently, slowly, they lowered him back down again. He closed his eyes, drifting.

He slept.

When he woke, he was alone. The calmness he had felt before he slept had gone. His shoulder throbbed and waves of heat swept over him. His skin twitched, his muscles jerked. He moved his head from side to side, for no reason that he knew.

Through the fevered thoughts, one stood strong and bright. That he had not finished the journey. There was more still to do. Perhaps, even, it was only the beginning.

The door opened. Soft footsteps across the room. A hand on his forehead. Knox, smiling with his clothlike skin, but never, never smiling with his eyes.

Robbie spoke, his mind suddenly quite clear, his voice like glass. "Do you remember me?"

"The boy with the injured hand? The boy who spied on me in my own house? Who gazed at my violin? The boy who picked up a knife, with God knows what intention? How could I forget you? And your questions." He gazed at the diamond ring on his finger, as he held the pulse in Robbie's wrist.

"No, from long ago. Six years ago."

"Should I?"

"My mother died."

"I know. You told me."

"You were the surgeon."

Robbie watched Knox's face. Saw a muscle in his cheek cringe. Felt the stillness of his body. For a long heavy moment, the earth stopped spinning.

Then Knox dropped Robbie's wrist, turned away, walked to the window. He looked smaller than Robbie remembered. His velvet jacket hung unevenly from his shoulders. When he turned back, Robbie saw that his watch chain was caught on a button and made two unbalanced loops. Vermilion streaked one cheek. "That is why you were outside my house," said Knox, in a level voice. "It was not the violin."

"I followed you," said Robbie. He continued, through the light veil of pain. "And that's why I mind, mind whose body you cut into. That's why I mind how those people died."

"And that is why I must not mind," said Knox, coming back toward him, his face framed by the moonlight now shafting through the window, his voice burning with a passion Robbie had never heard. He spoke to Robbie, spoke to him properly. "It is a choice I have made. Because if I minded, nothing would ever be learnt. I mind about curing people, any people. What else is my life about but that? I saved you. And I have saved countless others. But I could not save your mother. I failed. I regret that most deeply. I regret every life I cannot save."

Robbie could not speak into the silence that followed. This was what he had waited for so long to hear. Dr. Knox was sorry. Yet it did not seem to be the most important thing any longer.

He was tired. Very tired. It hurt to talk, but he had to ask. He turned toward Knox. "I heard you say something once. You said pain was God's will." He began to feel faint. "That it was wrong . . . to try . . . to take it away." He was exhausted.

Silence, followed by a roar of laughter. "Good God, you make me sound like a Calvinist minister!" His voice took on a mocking quality, as if playacting. "A shocking idea, quite shocking. To eliminate pain? Pain is God's will, His gift! How could we mortals be so audacious as to consider going against God's will? We should welcome pain, as God's gift to us."

"That was it!" gasped Robbie. "I heard you."

"You heard me!" agreed Knox, still smiling. "You heard me mocking the views of those pious fools who think God would put us on this earth to suffer. God put us on this earth to exercise our own free will, to make choices and to live by them. I am a surgeon. Everything I do is designed with one thing in mind, and one thing only—to find ways to cure patients. When they die, I have failed. I failed your mother. I am sorry."

The memory of his mother floated by, her soft hair trailing, the way she used to stroke his forehead, to kiss him every night, to say she loved him. The way when she smiled, a tiny dimple appeared on one cheek only. The sunlit apple-warm smell of her. The way she held him and never, never, never let him go. And the sparkle in her eyes. How could he have forgotten the fire-bright sparkle in her eyes?

Knox was sorry. It was what Robbie wanted. But did it matter? What did it matter what Dr. Knox did? It only mattered what he did himself. What choices he made. His mother had said, "In some things we just have no choice. In others we do. It is telling the difference that matters. You cannot choose what happens to you. But you can choose how to live. You can choose who to be."

Joseph came into the room with Essie. Through the fragile strength of her bright magpie eyes, she watched Robbie carefully and when he smiled, she smiled too, a tiny dimple on one cheek only. How had he never noticed that before?

11

A Few Years Later

Another summer humming toward its hazy end. In the distance the heathered hills, a faraway blush. A hanging sun warming the city.

Some students, laughing, clutching their books. All in black coats, sharp white collars, carefully rumpled cravats pushing their chins high.

A building with spires that stretched into the misty blue. Carvings, intricate patterns, an impossibly symmetrical design of arches and curves. A doorway, enormous. From the doorway, a young man, perhaps twenty, perhaps slightly more, hurrying down the steps. A kindly face, but focusing on something important inside himself.

Another man, a little younger, perhaps eighteen, something burning in his eager eyes, running down the steps after him. The younger man overtaking the other, running in front of him, stopping him with a hand on his arm.

Robbie spoke. "Sir, please, Dr. Simpson, sir."

The other man stopped, turned toward this student. He smiled, waited, as though he could spare any amount of time.

"I was at your lecture. I need to ask. What you were saying in there, sir. About surgery without pain, about patients being asleep while they are operated on. Do you really believe it is possible? In our lifetime?"

Dr. Simpson smiled. "Of course I do. It is what I am working on. It will happen one day, mark my words. And, God willing, I will be there when it does."

"Will you let me help you, sir?"

Dr. Simpson looked at him, considering. Then smiled. "Would you like to help me now? I am meeting some colleagues. We have been trying a miraculous substance that sends us into a deep sleep from which needles and any manner of pain will not wake us. But we must try it many times on different people, because the required dosage seems to vary. Are you willing?"

"Certainly, sir!" Robbie's heart flew. Clutching his books to his chest, he walked away with the young man, burning with questions.

Epilogue

Many Years Later—Edinburgh, 1862

The elderly surgeon, distinguished-looking, walked down the marbled corridor, calmly. He opened the thick heavy door at the end. The hum of many voices rose, and fell as he entered.

The surgeon removed his jacket and rolled up his sleeves. He washed his hands roughly. Dried them on a cloth that had been clean only the day before.

He walked over to the table set in the middle of the room. A wooden table. Nearby, some bottles, cloths, metal instruments. He smiled at the patient lying on the table, covered modestly by a sheet. She looked nervous, her face sheeny with sweat. "Do not be frightened," he said. She closed her eyes and unclenched her hands. A muscle in her face softened.

There was silence in the room. Though when you listened, focused, you could hear breathing, the occasional rustle, and distant sounds, birds, carriages, a train, a city calling. A tiny clink of metal on metal as the surgeon sorted the instruments. The sunlight danced drowsily on the walls. A cobweb hung across the ceiling, a spider watching.

The door opened. Footsteps across the floor. The surgeon looked up. A man was coming toward him, his face serious. All eyes turned toward the man. He whispered something in the surgeon's ear. The surgeon's shoulders slumped. Silence. He stared at the knife in his palm.

"Is everything all right, sir? Dr. Anderson?"

The surgeon looked up. "Yes, thank you. Thank you, yes. It is only that I have heard some bad news. Someone I knew, a long time ago, has died. He became a good friend."

Taking a deep breath, he smiled again at the patient. "Now, let us begin." She shrank. "Be calm. You will feel nothing. I shall put this over your face. Just breathe in as deeply as you can." He held a cloth in front of her, dripped some drops of colorless liquid from a bottle. Turning aside himself, holding his breath, he held it gently over her mouth and nose. Her muscles relaxed into a peaceful drifting faraway smile. He lifted back the sheet.

As Robbie sliced smoothly into the soft flesh, calmly, carefully, holding the razor-thin blade firmly, strongly, he heard it: floating somewhere above the woman's faraway dreaming, rising and falling, like the last song a swan might sing, the distant arpeggio of a violin.

Author's Note

Dr. Robert Knox was the real surgeon who bought the murdered victims from Burke and Hare. No one ever proved one way or the other whether he had known or suspected that they were murdered, but after the crimes were exposed, the mob was furious and attacked his house. He stayed in Edinburgh for some years, but his career was ruined, and he left for London, where he spent the rest of his life caring for cancer patients, often working amongst the poor and charging no fee. He did play the violin expertly, and his love of music was one of the many cultured aspects of his life. His arrogance made him many enemies—such as Professor James Syme, his perpetual rival—but his brilliance as an anatomist, surgeon and lecturer made him many friends and admirers.

Professor James Young Simpson is famous for his pioneering work with chloroform, for use in surgery as well as childbirth. He fought against the belief that pain in childbirth was God's will, His punishment to women for their disgrace in the Garden of Eden. Many times he was found unconscious on the floor after experimenting with ether and chloroform with his friends and colleagues.

The debt we owe to these surgeons and inventors is boundless. The admiration we should have for the patients is immense. They dared to be operated on without anesthetic, knowing that there was a very good chance of dying. Only through such sacrifice were the surgeons able to increase their knowledge of disease and the human body.

The scene I describe at the beginning of this book is closely based on a true story. I dedicate my story to that woman.

N.M.

About the Author

"I have always loved writing," Nicola Morgan says. "I am fascinated by the effects of words—how choosing a slightly different word can conjure an entirely different spell. Language is much more important than mere communication. It's what makes humans different from other animals. Stories are important, but much more important and interesting is how a story is told.

"I spent a *very* long time trying to write a novel that was good enough to be published. The eventual publication of *Mondays Are Red* was the realization of a dream. It was life-changing. Then, of course, I simply had to do it again, so here is *Fleshmarket,* a very different book. It was inspired by my taking a tour round Surgeons' Hall in Edinburgh and hearing the true and truly chilling story that forms the basis for the opening chapter. It grew into the story of *Fleshmarket* when I asked myself, as all writers do, 'What if . . . ?'

"I love writing for teenagers, young people, young adults, whatever you want to call them. They are open to new ideas, they can cope with a multilayered story, they respond to unusual language, they question, they demand to understand, and at the same time their imaginations are still free. In their imaginations, they can fly. For a writer, that is an unmissable opportunity."

Nicola Morgan lives with her family near Edinburgh.
You can visit her Web site at www.nicolamorgan.co.uk.